"If I Tried To Kiss You Right Now, You Wouldn't Stop Me."

The thought of Coop leaning over the console and pressing his lips to hers made her heart flutter and her stomach bottom out. But she squared her shoulders and said, "If you tried to kiss me, I'd deck you."

He threw his head back and laughed.

"You don't think I would do it?"

"No, you probably would, just to prove how tough you are. Then you would give in and let me kiss you anyway."

"The depth of your arrogance is truly remarkable."

"It's one of my most charming qualities," he said, but his grin said that he was definitely teasing her this time.

Maybe the confidence was a smoke screen, or this was his way of testing the waters. Maybe he really liked her, but being so used to women throwing themselves at him, the possibility of being rejected scared him.

Weirdly enough, the idea that under the tough-guy exterior there could be a vulnerable man made him that much more appealing.

Dear Reader,

I have a confession to make. I don't like sports.

Yes, you read that right. I don't like them. Baseball, football, hockey, soccer...they all bore me to tears. I don't even watch the Olympics. Which is why it makes no sense that I *love* romance novels with sports-playing heroes, and why I decided, after twenty-eight books, to finally write one myself. And frankly, if Cooper Landon could climb off the page and actually play hockey, I'd probably learn to love the game. Because let's face it, what could be sexier or more heartwarming than a big, tough—and let's not forget clueless—guy falling for a pair of adorable infant twin girls?

That's probably why Sierra Evans, who's not so crazy about sports herself, or men like Coop, can't resist him. Especially when the twins are her own daughters—a fact that she left out when she took the position as their nanny. But the closer she and Coop become, she knows that eventually the truth will have to come out. Still there are some secrets, devastating ones, that must stay hidden away forever or it could mean never seeing her daughters again.

Until next time,

Michelle

The Nanny Bombshell

MICHELLE CELMER

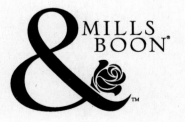

First published in Great Britain 2012
by Mills & Boon, an imprint of Harlequin (UK) Limited.
Large Print edition 2012
Harlequin (UK) Limited,
Eton House, 18-24 Paradise Road,
Richmond, Surrey TW9 1SR

© Michelle Celmer 2012

ISBN: 978 0 263 22977 6

Printed and bound in Great Britain
by CPI Antony Rowe, Chippenham, Wiltshire

MICHELLE CELMER

Bestselling author Michelle Celmer lives in southeastern Michigan with her husband, their three children, two dogs and two cats. When she's not writing or busy being a mom, you can find her in the garden or curled up with a romance novel. And if you twist her arm really hard, you can usually persuade her into a day of power shopping.

Michelle loves to hear from readers. Visit her website, www.michellecelmer.com, or write her at P.O. Box 300, Clawson, MI 48017.

To my granddaughter,
Aubrey Helen Ann

One

This was not good.

As a former defensive center, MVP and team captain for the New York Scorpions, Cooper Landon was one of the city's most beloved sports heroes. His hockey career had never been anything but an asset.

Until today.

He looked out the conference room window in the Manhattan office of his attorney, where he had been parked for the past ninety minutes, hands wedged in the pockets of his jeans, watching the late afternoon traffic crawl along Park Avenue. The early June sun reflected with a blinding intensity off the windows of the building across the street and the sidewalks were clogged with people going about their daily routine. Businessmen catching cabs, mothers pushing strollers. Three weeks ago he'd been one of them, walking through life oblivious to how quickly his world could be turned completely upside down.

One senseless accident had robbed him of the only family he had. Now his brother, Ash, and sister-in-law, Susan, were dead, and his twin infant nieces were orphans.

He clenched his fists, fighting back the anger and injustice of it, when what he wanted to do was slam them through the tinted glass.

He still had his nieces, he reminded himself. Though they had been adopted, Ash and Susan couldn't have loved them more if they were their own flesh and blood. Now they were Coop's responsibility, and he was determined to do right by them, give them the sort of life his brother wanted them to have. He owed Ash.

"So, what did you think of that last one?" Ben Hearst, his attorney, asked him. He sat at the conference table sorting through the applications and taking notes on the nanny candidates they had seen that afternoon.

Coop turned to him, unable to mask his frustration. "I wouldn't trust her to watch a hamster."

Like the three other women they had interviewed that day, the latest applicant had been more interested in his hockey career than talking about the twins. He'd met her type a million times before. In her short skirt and low-cut blouse, she was looking to land herself a famous husband. Though in the past he would have enjoyed the attention and, yeah, he probably would have taken advantage of it, now he found it annoying. He wasn't seen as the guardian of two precious girls who lost their parents, but as a piece of meat. He'd lost his brother two weeks ago and not a single nanny candidate had thought to offer their condolences.

After two days and a dozen equally unproductive interviews, he was beginning to think he would never find the right nanny.

His housekeeper, who had been grudgingly

helping him with the twins and was about twenty years past her child-rearing prime, had threatened to quit if he didn't find someone else to care for them.

"I'm really sorry," Ben said. "I guess we should have anticipated this happening."

Maybe Coop should have taken Ben's advice and used a service. He just didn't feel that a bunch of strangers would be qualified to choose the person who would be best to care for the twins.

"I think you're going to like this next one," Ben told him.

"Is she qualified?"

"Overqualified, actually." He handed Coop the file. "You could say that I was saving the best for last."

Sierra Evans, twenty-six. She had graduated from college with a degree in nursing, and it listed her current occupation as a pediatric nurse. Coop blinked, then looked at Ben. "Is this right?"

He smiled and nodded. "I was surprised, too."

She was single and childless with a clean record. She didn't have so much as a parking ticket. On paper she looked perfect. Although in his experience, if something seemed too good to be true, it usually was. "What's the catch?"

Ben shrugged. "Maybe there isn't one. She's waiting in the lobby. You ready to meet her?"

"Let's do it," he said, feeling hopeful for the first time since this whole mess started. Maybe this one would be as good as she sounded.

Using the intercom, Ben asked the receptionist, "Would you send Miss Evans in please?"

A minute later the door opened and a woman walked in. Immediately Coop could see that she was different from the others. She was dressed in scrubs—dark-blue pants and a white top with Sesame Street characters all over it—and comfortable-looking shoes. Not typical attire for a job interview but a decided improvement over the clingy, revealing choices of her predecessors. She was average height, average build...very unremarkable. But her face, that was anything but average.

Her eyes were so dark brown they looked

black and a slight tilt in the corners gave her an Asian appearance. Her mouth was wide, lips full and sensual, and though she didn't wear a stitch of makeup, she didn't need any. Her black hair was long and glossy and pulled back in a slightly lopsided ponytail.

One thing was clear. This woman was no groupie.

"Miss Evans," Ben said, rising to shake her hand. "I'm Ben Hearst, and this is Cooper Landon."

Coop gave her a nod but stayed put in his place by the window.

"I apologize for the scrubs," she said in a voice that was on the husky side. "I came straight from work."

"It's not a problem," Ben assured her, gesturing to a chair. "Please, have a seat."

She sat, placing her purse—a nondesigner bag that had seen better days—on the table beside her and folded her hands in her lap. Coop stood silently observing as Ben launched into the litany of questions he'd asked every candidate. She dutifully answered every one of them, darting glances Coop's way every so often but keeping her attention on Ben. The others had asked Coop questions, tried to engage him in conversation. But from Miss Evans there was no starry-eyed gazing, no flirting or innuendo. No smoldering smiles and suggestions that she would do *anything* for the job. In fact, she avoided his gaze, as if his presence made her nervous.

"You understand that this is a live-in position. You will be responsible for the twins 24/7. 11:00 a.m. to 4:00 p.m. on Sundays, and every fourth weekend from Saturday at 8:00 a.m. to Sunday at 8:00 p.m., is yours to spend as you wish," Ben said.

She nodded. "I understand."

Ben turned to Coop. "Do you have anything to add?"

"Yeah, I do." He addressed Miss Evans directly. "Why would you give up a job as a pediatric nurse to be a nanny?"

"I love working with kids...obviously," she said with a shy smile—a pretty smile. "But working in the neonatal intensive care unit is a very high-stress job. It's emotionally drain-ing. I need a change of pace. And I can't deny that the live-in situation is alluring."

A red flag began to wave furiously. "Why is that?"

"My dad is ill and unable to care for him-self. The salary you're offering, along with not having to pay rent, would make it possible for me to put him in a top-notch facility. In fact, there's a place in Jersey that has a spot opening up this week, so the timing would be perfect."

That was the last thing he had expected her to say, and for a second he was speechless. He didn't know of many people, especially some-one in her tax bracket, who would sacrifice such a large chunk of their salary for the care of a parent. Even Ben looked a little surprised.

He shot Coop a look that asked, *What do you think?* As things stood, Coop couldn't come up with a single reason not to hire her on the spot, but he didn't want to act rashly. This was about the girls, not his personal convenience.

"I'd like you to come by and meet my nieces tomorrow," he told her.

She regarded him hopefully. "Does that mean I have the job?"

"I'd like to see you interact with them before I make the final decision, but I'll be honest, you're by far the most qualified candidate we've seen so far."

"Tomorrow is my day off so I can come anytime."

"Why don't we say 1:00 p.m., after the girls' lunch. I'm a novice at this parenting thing, so it usually takes me until then to get them bathed, dressed and fed."

She smiled. "One is fine."

"I'm on the Upper East Side. Ben will give you the address."

Ben jotted down Coop's address and handed it to her. She took the slip of paper and tucked it into her purse.

Ben stood, and Miss Evans rose to her feet. She grabbed her purse and slung it over her shoulder.

"One more thing, Miss Evans," Coop said. "Are you a hockey fan?"

She hesitated. "Um…is it a prerequisite for the job?"

He felt a smile tugging at the corner of his mouth. "Of course not."

"Then, no, not really. I've never much been into sports. Although I was in a bowling league in college. Until recently my dad was a pretty big hockey fan, though."

"So you know who I am?"

"Is there anyone in New York who doesn't?"

Probably not, and only recently had that fact become a liability. "That isn't going to be an issue?"

She cocked her head slightly. "I'm not sure what you mean."

Her confusion made him feel like an idiot for even asking. Was he so used to women fawning over him that he'd come to expect it? Maybe he wasn't her type, or maybe she had a boy-friend. "Never mind."

She turned to leave, then paused and turned back to him.

"I wanted to say, I was so sorry to hear about

your brother and his wife. I know how hard it is to lose someone you love."

The sympathy in her dark eyes made him want to squirm, and that familiar knot lodged somewhere in the vicinity of his Adam's apple. It annoyed him when the others hadn't mentioned it, but when she did, it made him uncomfortable. Maybe because she seemed as though she really meant it.

"Thank you," he said. He'd certainly had his share of loss. First his parents when he was twelve, and now Ash and Susan. Maybe that was the price he had to pay for fame and success.

He would give it all up, sell his soul if that was what it took to get his brother back.

After she left Ben asked him, "So, you really think she's the one?"

"She's definitely qualified, and it sounds as though she needs the job. As long as the girls like her, I'll offer her the position."

"Easy on the eyes, too."

He shot Ben a look. "If I manage to find a nanny worth hiring, do you honestly think I would risk screwing it up by getting physically involved?"

Ben smirked. "Honestly?"

Okay, a month ago…maybe. But everything had changed since then.

"I prefer blondes," he told Ben. "The kind with no expectations and questionable morals."

Besides, taking care of the girls, seeing that they were raised in the manner Ash and Susan would want, was his top priority. Coop owed his brother that much. When their parents died, Ash had only been eighteen, but he'd put his own life on hold to raise Coop. And Coop hadn't made it easy at first. He'd been hurt and confused and had lashed out. He was out of control and fast on his way to becoming a full-fledged juvenile delinquent when the school psychologist told Ash that Coop needed a constructive outlet for his anger. She suggested a physical sport, so Ash had signed him up for hockey.

Coop had never been very athletic or interested in sports, but he took to the game instantly, and though he was on a team with kids who had been playing since they were old enough to balance on skates, he rapidly surpassed their skills. Within two years he was playing in a travel league and became the star player. At nineteen he was picked up by the New York Scorpions.

A knee injury two years ago had cut his career short, but smart investments—again thanks to the urging of his brother—had left him wealthy beyond his wildest dreams. Without Ash, and the sacrifices he made, it never would have been possible. Now Coop had the chance to repay him. But he couldn't do it alone. He was ill-equipped. He knew nothing about caring for an infant, much less two at once. Hell, until two weeks ago he'd never so much as changed a diaper. Without his housekeeper to help, he would be lost.

If Miss Evans turned out to be the right person for the job—and he had the feeling she was—he would never risk screwing it up by sleeping with her.

She was off-limits.

* * *

Sierra Evans rode the elevator down to the lobby of the attorney's office building, sagging with relief against the paneled wall. That had gone much better than she could have hoped and she was almost positive that the job was as good as hers. It was a good thing, too, because the situation was far worse than she could have imagined.

Clearly Cooper Landon had better things to do than care for his twin nieces. He was probably too busy traipsing around like the playboy of the Western world. She wasn't one to listen to gossip, but in his case, his actions and reputation as a womanizing partier painted a disturbing picture. That was not the kind of atmosphere in which she wanted her daughters raised.

Her daughters. Only recently had she begun thinking of them as hers again.

With Ash and Susan gone, it seemed wrong that the twins would be so carelessly pawned off on someone like Cooper. But she would save them. She would take care of them and love them. It was all that mattered now.

The doors slid open and she stepped out. She crossed the swanky lobby and pushed out the door into the sunshine, heading down Park Avenue in the direction of the subway, feeling hopeful for the first time in two weeks.

Giving the twins up had been the hardest thing she'd ever done in her life, but she knew it was for the best. Between her student loans and exorbitant rent, not to mention her dad's failing health and mounting medical bills, she was in no position financially or emotionally to care for infant twins. She knew that Ash and Susan, the girls' adoptive parents, would give her babies everything that she couldn't.

But in the blink of an eye they were gone. She had been standing in front of the television, flipping through the channels when she paused on the news report about the plane crash. When she realized it was Ash and Susan they were talking about, her knees had buckled and she'd dropped to the nubby, threadbare shag carpet. In a panic she had flipped through the channels, desperate for more details, terrified to the depths of her soul that the girls had been on the flight with them. She'd sat up all night, alternating between the television and her laptop, gripped by a fear and a soul-wrenching grief that had been all-consuming.

At 7:00 a.m. the following morning the early news confirmed that the girls had in fact been left with Susan's family and were not in the crash. Sierra had been so relieved she wept. But then the reality of the situation hit hard. Who would take the girls? Would they go to Susan's family permanently or, God forbid, be dropped into the foster-care system?

She had contacted her lawyer immediately, and after a few calls he had learned what to her was unthinkable. Cooper would be their guardian. What the hell had Ash been thinking, choosing him? What possible interest could a womanizing, life of the party, ex-hockey player have in two infant babies?

She'd asked her lawyer to contact him on her behalf using no names, assuming that he would be more than happy to give the girls back to their natural mother. She would find a way to make it work. But Cooper had refused to give them up.

Her lawyer said she could try to fight him for custody, but the odds weren't in her favor. She had severed her parental rights, and getting them back would take a lengthy and expensive legal battle. But knowing Cooper would undoubtedly need help, and would probably be thrilled with someone of her qualifications, she'd managed to get herself an interview for the nanny position.

Sierra boarded the subway at Lexington and took the F Train to Queens. Normally she visited her dad on Wednesdays, but she had the appointment at Cooper's apartment tomorrow so she had to rearrange her schedule. With any luck he would offer her the job on the spot, and she could go home and start packing immediately.

She took a cab from the station to the dumpy, third-rate nursing home where her dad had spent the past fourteen months. As she passed the nursing station she said hi to the nurse seated there and received a grunt of annoyance in return. She would think that being in the same profession there would be some semblance of professional courtesy, but the opposite was true. The nurses seemed to resent her presence.

She hated that her dad had to stay in this horrible place where the employees were apathetic and the care was borderline criminal, but this was all that Medicare would cover and home care at this late stage of the disease was just too expensive. His body had lost the ability to perform anything but the most basic functions. He couldn't speak, barely reacted to stimuli and had to be fed through a tube. His heart was still beating, his lungs still pulling in air, but eventually his body would forget how to do that, too. It could be weeks, or months. He might even linger on for a year or more. There was just no way to know. If she could get him into the place in Jersey it would be harder to visit, but at least he would be well cared for.

"Hi, Lenny." She greeted her dad's roommate, a ninety-one-year-old war vet who had lost his right foot and his left arm in the battle at Normandy.

"Hey there, Sierra," he said cheerfully from his wheelchair. He was dressed in dark brown pants and a Kelly-green cardigan sweater that were as old and tattered as their wearer.

"How is Dad today?" she asked, dropping her purse in the chair and walking to his bedside. It broke her heart to see him so shriveled and lifeless. Nothing more than a shell of the man he used to be—the loving dad who single-handedly raised Sierra and her little sister Joy. Now he was wasting away.

"It's been a good day," Lenny said.

"Hi, Daddy," she said, pressing a kiss to his papery cheek. He was awake, but he didn't acknowledge her. On a good day he lay quietly, either sleeping or staring at the dappled sunshine through the dusty vertical blinds. On a bad day, he moaned. A low, tortured, unearthly sound. They didn't know if he was in pain, or if it was just some random involuntary function. But on those days he was sedated.

"How is that little boy of yours?" Lenny asked. "Must be reaching about school age by now."

She sighed softly to herself. Lenny's memory wasn't the best. He somehow managed to remember that she'd been pregnant, but he forgot the dozen or so times when she had explained that she'd given the girls up for adoption. And clearly he was confusing her with other people in his life because sometimes he thought she had an older boy and other times it was a baby girl. And rather than explain yet again, she just went with it.

"Growing like a weed," she told him, and before he could ask more questions they announced over the intercom that it was time for bingo in the community room.

"Gotta go!" Lenny said, wheeling himself toward the door. "Can I bring you back a cookie?"

"No thanks, Lenny."

When he was gone she sat on the edge of her dad's bed and took his hand. It was cold and contracted into a stiff fist. "I had my job interview today," she told him, even though she doubted his brain could process the sounds he was hearing as anything but gibberish. "It went really well, and I get to see the girls tomorrow. If the other applicants looked anything like the bimbo who interviewed right before me, I'm a shoo-in."

She brushed a few silvery strands of hair back from his forehead. "I know you're probably thinking that I should stay out of this and trust Ash and Susan's judgment, but I just can't. The man is a train wreck just waiting to happen. I have to make sure the girls are okay. If I can't do that as their mother, I can at least do it as their nanny."

And if that meant sacrificing her freedom and working for Cooper Landon until the girls no longer needed her, that was what she was prepared to do.

Two

The next afternoon at six minutes after one, Sierra knocked on the door of Cooper's penthouse apartment, brimming with nervous excitement, her heart in her throat. She had barely slept last night in anticipation of this very moment. Though she had known that when she signed away her parental rights she might never see the girls again, she had still hoped. She just hadn't expected it to happen until they were teenagers and old enough to make the decision to meet their birth mother. But here she was, barely five months later, just seconds away from the big moment.

The door was opened by a woman. Sierra assumed it was the housekeeper, judging by the maid's uniform. She was tall and lanky with a pinched face and steel-gray hair that was pulled back severely and twisted into a bun. Sierra placed her in her mid to late sixties.

"Can I *help* you?" the woman asked in a gravely clipped tone.

"I have an appointment with Mr. Landon."

"Are you Miss Evans?"

"Yes, I am." Which she must have already known, considering the doorman had called up to announce her about a minute ago.

She looked Sierra up and down with scrutiny, pursed her lips and said, "I'm Ms. Densmore, Mr. Landon's housekeeper. You're late."

"Sorry. I had trouble getting a cab."

"I should warn you that if you do get the job, tardiness will not be tolerated."

Sierra failed to see how she could be tardy for a job she was at 24/7, but she didn't push the issue. "It won't happen again."

Ms. Densmore gave a resentful sniff and said, "Follow me."

Even the housekeeper's chilly greeting wasn't enough to smother Sierra's excitement. Her hands trembled as she followed her through the foyer into an ultra-modern, open-concept living space. Near a row of ceiling-high windows that boasted a panoramic view of Central Park, with the afternoon sunshine washing over them like gold dust, were the twins. They sat side by side in identical ExerSaucers, babbling and swatting at the colorful toys.

They were so big! And they had changed more than she could have imagined possible. If she had seen them on the street, she probably wouldn't have recognized them. She was hit by a sense of longing so keen she had to bite down on her lip to keep from bursting into tears. She forced her feet to remain rooted to the deeply polished mahogany floor while she was announced, when what she wanted to do was fling herself into the room, drop down to her knees and gather her children in her arms.

"The one on the left is Fern," Ms. Densmore said, with not a hint of affection in her tone.

"She's the loud, demanding one. The other is Ivy. She's the quiet, sneaky one."

Sneaky? At five months old? It sounded as if Ms. Densmore just didn't like children. She was probably a spinster. She sure looked like one.

Not only would Sierra have to deal with a partying, egomaniac athlete, but also an overbearing and critical housekeeper. How fun. And it frosted her that Cooper let this pinched, frigid, nasty old bat who clearly didn't like children anywhere near the girls.

"I'll go get Mr. Landon," she said, striding down a hall that Sierra assumed led to the bedrooms.

Alone with her girls for the first time since their birth, she crossed the room and knelt down in front of them. "Look how big you are, and how beautiful," she whispered.

They gazed back at her with wide, inquisitive blue eyes. Though they weren't identical, they looked very much alike. They both had her thick, pin-straight black hair and high cheekbones, but any other traces of the Chinese traits that had come from her great-grandmother on her mother's side had skipped them. They had eyes just like their father and his long, slender fingers.

Fern let out a squeal and reached for her. Sierra wanted so badly to hold her, but she wasn't sure if she should wait for Cooper. Tears stinging her eyes, she took one of Fern's chubby little hands in hers and held it. She had missed them so much, and the guilt she felt for leaving them, for putting them in this situation, sat like a stone in her belly. But she was here now, and she would never leave them again. She would see that they were raised properly.

"She wants you to pick her up."

Sierra turned to see Cooper standing several feet behind her, big and burly, in bare feet with his slightly wrinkled shirt untucked and his hands wedged in the pockets of a pair of threadbare jeans. His dirty-blond hair was damp and a little messy, as if he'd towel-dried it and hadn't bothered with a brush. No one could deny that he was attractive with his pale blue eyes and dimpled smile. The slightly crooked nose was even a little charming. Maybe it was his total lack of self-consciousness that was so appealing right now, but athletes had never been her thing. She preferred studious men. Professional types. The kind who didn't make a living swinging a big stick and beating the crap out of other people.

"Do you mind?" she asked.

"Of course not. That's what this interview is about."

Sierra lifted Fern out of the seat and set the infant in her lap. She smelled like baby shampoo and powder. Fern fixated on the gold chain hanging down the front of her blouse and grabbed for it, so Sierra tucked it under her collar. "She's so big."

"Around fifteen pounds I think. I remember my sister-in-law saying that they were average size for their age. I'm not sure what they weighed when they were born. I think there's a baby book still packed away somewhere with all that information in it."

They had been just over six pounds each, but she couldn't tell him that or that the baby book he referred to had been started by her and given to Ash and Susan as a gift when they took the girls home. She had documented her entire pregnancy—when she felt the first kick, when she had her sonogram—so the adoptive parents would feel more involved and they could show the girls when they got older. And although she had included photos of her belly in various stages of development, there were no shots of her face. There was nothing anywhere that identified her as being the birth mother.

Ivy began to fuss—probably jealous that her sister was getting all the attention. Sierra was debating the logistics of how to extract her from the seat while still holding Fern when, without prompting, Cooper reached for Ivy and plucked her out. He lifted her high over his head, making her gasp and giggle, and plunked her down in his arms.

Sierra must have looked concerned because he laughed and said, "Don't let her mild manner fool you. She's a mini daredevil."

As he sat on the floor across from her and set Ivy in his lap, Sierra caught the scent of some sort of masculine soap. Fern reached for him and tried to wiggle her way out of Sierra's arms. She hadn't expected the girls to be so at ease with him, so attached. Not this quickly. And she expected him to be much more inept and disinterested.

"You work with younger babies?" Cooper asked.

"Newborns usually. But before the NICU I worked in the pediatric ward."

"I'm going to the market," Ms. Densmore announced from the kitchen. Sierra had been so focused on the girls she hadn't noticed that it was big and open with natural wood and frosted glass cupboard doors and yards of glossy granite countertops. Modern, yet functional—not that she ever spent much time in one. Cooking—or at least, cooking *well*—had never been one of her great accomplishments.

Ms. Densmore wore a light spring jacket, which was totally unnecessary considering it was at least seventy-five degrees outside, and clutched an old-lady-style black handbag. "Do you need anything?" she asked Cooper.

"Diapers and formula," he told her. "And those little jars of fruit the girls like." He paused, then added, "And the dried cereal, too. The flaky kind in the blue box. I think we're running low."

Looking annoyed, Ms. Densmore left out of what must have been the service entrance behind the kitchen. Sierra couldn't help but wonder how Coop would know the cereal was low and why he would even bother to look.

"The girls are eating solid foods?" she asked him.

"Cereal and fruit. And of course formula. It's astounding how much they can put away. I feel as if I'm constantly making bottles."

He made the bottles? She had a hard time picturing that. Surely Ms. Cranky-Pants must have been doing most of the work.

"Are they sleeping through the night?" she asked him.

"Not yet. It's getting better, though. At first, they woke up constantly." He smiled down at Ivy affectionately, and a little sadly, brushing a wisp of hair off her forehead. "I think they just really missed their parents. But last night they only woke up twice, and they both went back to their cribs. Half the time they end up in my bed with me. I'll admit that I'm looking forward to a good night's sleep. Alone."

"*You* get up with them?" she asked, not meaning to sound quite so incredulous.

Rather than look offended, he smiled. "Yeah, and I'll warn you right now that they're both bed hogs. I have no idea how a person so small could take up so much room."

The idea of him, such a big, burly, rough-around-the-edges guy, snuggled up in bed with two infants, was too adorable for words.

"Out of curiosity, who did you think would get up with them?" he asked.

"I just assumed... I mean, doesn't Ms. Densmore take care of them?"

"She occasionally watches them while I work, but only because I'm desperate. After raising six kids of her own and two of her grandchildren, she says she's finished taking care of babies."

So much for Sierra's spinster theory.

"Is she always so…" She struggled for a kind way to say *nasty,* but Cooper seemed to read her mind.

"Cranky? Incorrigible?" he suggested, with a slightly crooked smile that she hated to admit made her heart beat the tiniest bit faster.

She couldn't help smiling back.

"She won't be winning any congeniality awards, I know, but she's a good housekeeper, and one hel…" he grinned and shook his head. "I mean *heck* of a fantastic cook. Sorry, I'm not used to having to censor my language."

At least he was making an effort. He would be thankful for that in a year or so when the twins started repeating everything he said verbatim.

"Ms. Densmore isn't crazy about the bad language, either," he said. "Of course, sometimes I do it just to annoy her."

"I don't think she likes me much," Sierra said.

"It really doesn't matter what she thinks. She's not hiring you. I am. And I happen to think you're perfect for the job." He paused then added, "I'm assuming, since you're here now, that you're still interested."

Her heart skipped a beat. "Absolutely. Does that mean you're officially offering it to me?"

"Under one condition—I need your word that you'll stick around. That you're invested in the position. I can't tell you how tough that first week was, right after…" He closed his eyes, took a deep breath and blew it out. "Things have just begun to settle down, and I've got the girls in something that resembles a routine. They need consistency—or at least that's what the social worker told me. The worst thing for them would be a string of nannies bouncing in and out of their lives."

He would never have to worry about that with her. "I won't let them down."

"You're *sure?* Because these two are a handful. It's a lot of work. More than I ever imagined possible. Professional hockey was a cakewalk compared to this. I need to be sure that you're committed."

"I'm giving up my apartment and putting my

dad in a home that I can't begin to afford without this salary. I'm definitely committed."

He looked relieved. "In that case, the job is yours. And the sooner you can start, the better."

Her own relief was so keen she could have sobbed. She hugged Fern closer. Her little girls would be okay. She would be there to take care of them, to nurture them. And maybe someday, when they were old enough to understand, she would be able to tell them who she really was and explain why she had let them go. Maybe she could be a real mother to them.

"Miss Evans?" Coop was watching her expectantly, waiting for a reply.

"It's Sierra," she told him. "And I can start right away if that works for you. I just need a day to pack and move my things in."

He looked surprised. "What about your apartment? Your furniture? Don't you need time to—"

"I'll sublet. A friend from work is interested in taking my place and she'll be using all my furniture." Her dad's furniture, actually. By the time Sierra started making enough money to afford her own place, he was too sick to live alone, so she had stayed with him instead, on the pull-out couch of the dinky one-bedroom apartment he'd had to take when he went on disability. She had never really had a place of her own. And from the looks of it, she wouldn't for a very long time. But if that meant the girls would be happy and well taken care of, it was a sacrifice she was happy to make.

"I just need to pack my clothes and a few personal items," she told him. "I can do that today and move everything over tomorrow."

"And work? You don't need to give them notice?"

She shook her head. She was taking a chance burning that bridge, but being with the girls as soon as possible took precedence. As long as they needed her, she wouldn't be going back to nursing anyway.

"I'll have Ben, my lawyer, draw up the contract this afternoon," he said. "Considering my former profession there are privacy issues."

"I understand."

"And of course you're welcome to have your own lawyer look at it before you sign."

"I'll call him today."

"Great. Why don't I show you the girls' room, and where you'll be staying?"

"Okay."

They got up from the floor and he led her down the hall, Ivy in his arms and Sierra holding Fern, who seemed perfectly content despite Sierra being a relative stranger. Was it possible that she sensed the mother-daughter connection? Or was she just a friendly, outgoing baby?

"This is the nursery," he said, indicating a door on the left and gesturing her inside. It was by far the largest and prettiest little girls' room she had ever laid eyes on. The color scheme was pale pink and pastel green. The walls, bedding, curtains and even the carpet looked fluffy and soft, like cotton candy. Matching white cribs perched side by side, and a white rocking chair sat in the corner next to the window. She could just imagine herself holding the girls close, singing them a lullaby and rocking them to sleep.

This room was exactly what she would have wanted for them but never could have afforded. With her they wouldn't have had more than a tiny corner of her bedroom.

"It's beautiful, Cooper."

"It's Coop," he said and flashed that easy grin. "No one but my mom called me Cooper, and that was usually when she was angry about something. And as for the room, I can't take credit. It's an exact reproduction of their room at Ash and Susan's. I thought it might make the transition easier for them."

Once again he had surprised her. Maybe he wasn't quite as self-centered as she first imagined. Or maybe he was only playing the role of responsible uncle out of necessity. Maybe once he had her there to take care of the girls for him, he would live up to his party reputation, including the supposedly revolving bedroom door.

Time would tell.

"They have their own bathroom and a walk-in closet over there," he said, gesturing to a closed door across the room.

She walked over and opened it. The closet was huge! Toys lined either side of the floor—things they had used and some still in the original boxes. Seeing them, Fern shifted restlessly in Sierra's arms, clearly wanting to get down and play.

From the bars hung a wardrobe big enough for a dozen infants. Dresses and jumpers and tiny pairs of jeans and shirts—all designer labels and many with the tags still attached, and all in duplicate. In her wildest dreams Sierra never could have afforded even close to this many clothes, and certainly not this quality. They were neatly organized by style, color and size—all spelled out on sticky notes on the shelf above the bar.

Sierra had never seen anything like it. "Wow. Did you do this?"

"God, no," Coop said. "This is Ms. Densmore's thing. She's a little fanatical about organization."

"Just a little." She would have a coronary if she looked in Sierra's closet. Besides being just a fraction the size, it was so piled with junk she could barely close the door. Neatness had never been one of her strong suits. That had been okay living with her dad, who was never tidy himself, but here she would have to make an effort to be more organized.

"The bathroom is through there," Coop said, walking past her to open the door, filling the air with the delicious scent of soap and man. The guy really did smell great, and though it was silly, he looked even more attractive holding the baby, which made no sense at all. Or maybe it was just that she'd always been a sucker for a man who was good with kids—because in her profession she had seen too many who weren't. Deadbeat dads who couldn't even be bothered to visit their sick child in the hospital. And of course there were the abusive dads who put their kids in the hospital. Those were the really heartbreaking cases and one of the reasons she had transferred from pediatrics to the NICU.

But having an easy way with an infant didn't make a man a good father, she reminded herself. Neither did giving them a big beautiful bedroom or an enormous closet filled with toys and designer clothes. The twins needed nurturing, they needed to know that even though their parents were gone, someone still loved them and cared about them.

She held Fern closer and rubbed her back, and the infant laid her head on Sierra's shoulder, her thumb tucked in her mouth.

"I'll show you your room," Coop said, and she followed him to the bedroom across the hall. It was even larger than the girls' room, with the added bonus of a cozy sitting area by the window. With the bedroom, walk-in closet and private bath, it was larger than her entire apartment. All that was missing was the tiny, galley-style kitchen, but she had a gourmet kitchen just a few rooms away at her disposal.

The furnishings and decor weren't exactly her style. The black, white and gray color scheme was too modern and cold and the steel and glass furnishings were a bit masculine, but bringing some of her own things in would liven it up a little. She could learn to live with it.

"That bad, huh?"

Startled by the comment, Sierra looked over at Coop. He was frowning. "I didn't say that."

"You didn't have to. It's written all over your face. You hate it."

"I don't *hate* it."

One brow tipped up. "Now you're lying."

"It's not what I would have chosen, but it's very… stylish."

He laughed. "You are *so* lying. You think it's terrible."

She bit her lip to keep from smiling, but the corners of her mouth tipped up regardless. "I'll get used to it."

"I'll call my decorator. You can fix it however you like. Paint, furniture, the works."

She opened her mouth to tell him that wouldn't be necessary, and he held up one ridiculously large palm to shush her. "Do you really think I'm going to let you stay in a room you despise? This is going to be your home. I want you to be comfortable here."

She wondered if he was always this nice, or if he was just so desperate for a reliable nanny he would do anything to convince her to take the job. If that was the case, she could probably negotiate a higher salary, but it wasn't about the money. She just wanted to be with her girls.

"If you're sure it's not a problem, I wouldn't mind adding a few feminine touches," she told him.

"You can sleep in the nursery until it's finished, or if you'd prefer more privacy, there's a fold-out love seat in my office."

"The nursery is fine." She didn't care about privacy, and she liked the idea of sleeping near her girls.

He nodded to Fern and said, "I think we should lay them down. It's afternoon nap time."

Sierra looked down at Fern and realized that she had fallen asleep, her thumb still wedged in her mouth, and Ivy, who had laid her head on Coop's enormously wide shoulder, was looking drowsy, too.

They carried the girls back to the nursery and laid them in their beds—Fern on the right side and Ivy on the left—then they stepped quietly out and Coop shut the door behind them.

"How long will they sleep?" Sierra asked.

"On a good day, two hours. But they slept in until eight this morning, so maybe less." He paused in the hall and asked, "Before we call my attorney, would you like something to drink? We have juice and soda...baby formula."

She smiled. "I'm good, thanks."

"Okay, if you're having any second thoughts, this is your last chance to change your mind."

That would never happen. He was stuck with her. "No second thoughts."

"Great, let's go to my office and call Ben," Coop said with a grin. "Let's get this show on the road."

<u>Three</u>

Coop stood outside Sierra's bedroom door, hoping she hadn't already gone to sleep for the night. It was barely nine-thirty, but today had been her first official day watching the girls, so he was guessing that she was probably pretty exhausted. God knows they wore him out.

She had signed the contract the afternoon of her second interview, then spent most of the next day moving her things and unpacking. He had offered to pay a service to do the moving for her, but she had insisted she had it covered, showing up in the early afternoon with a slew of boxes and two youngish male friends—orderlies from the hospital, she'd told him—who had been openly thrilled to meet the great Coop Landon.

Though Coop had tried to pay them for the help, they refused to take any cash. Instead he offered them each a beer, and while Sierra unpacked and the twins napped, he and the guys sat out on the rooftop patio. They asked him about his career and the upcoming season draft picks, leaving a couple of hours later with autographed pucks.

Coop had hoped to be around today to help Sierra and the twins make the transition, but he'd been trapped in meetings with the marketing team for his new sports equipment line all morning, and in the afternoon he'd met with the owner of his former team. If things went as planned, Coop would own the team before the start of the next season in October. Owning the New York Scorpions had been his dream since he started playing for the team. For twenty-two years, until his bad knee took him off the ice, he lived and breathed hockey. He loved everything about the game. Buying a team was the natural next step, and he had the players' blessing.

After the meetings Coop had enjoyed his first dinner out with friends in weeks. Well, he hadn't actually *enjoyed* it. Though he had been counting the days until he was free again, throughout the entire meal his mind kept wandering back to Fern and Ivy and how they were doing with Sierra. Should he have canceled his meetings and spent that first day with them? Was it irresponsible of him to have left them with a stranger? Not that he didn't trust Sierra—he just wanted to be sure that he was doing the right thing. They had already lost their parents—he didn't want them to think that he was abandoning them, too.

When the rest of the party had moved on to a local bar for after-dinner drinks, dancing and skirt chasing, to the surprise of his friends, Coop had called it a night. On a typical evening he closed out the bar, moved on to a party and usually didn't go home alone. But the ribbing he endured from his buddies was mild. Hell, it had been less than a month since he lost his brother. It was going to take him a little time to get back into his normal routine. And right now the twins needed him. He would try to work from home the rest of the week, so he could spend more time with them. After more than two weeks of being together almost constantly, he had gotten used to having them around.

He rapped lightly on Sierra's bedroom door, and after several seconds it opened a crack and she peeked out. He could see that she had already changed into her pajamas—a short, pink, babydoll-style nightgown. His eyes automatically drifted lower, to her bare legs. They weren't particularly long, or slender, so the impulse to touch her, to slide his palm up the inside of one creamy thigh and under the hem of her gown—and the resulting pull of lust it created—caught him completely off guard. He had to make an effort to keep his gaze above her neck and on her eyes, which were dark and inquisitive, with that exotic tilt. Her hair, which he'd only ever seen up in a ponytail, hung in a long, silky black sheet over her shoulders, and he itched to run his fingers through it. Instead he shoved his hands in the pockets of his slacks.

You can look, but you can't touch, he reminded himself, and not for the first time since she'd come by to meet the girls. She was absolutely nothing like the sort of woman he would typically be attracted to. Maybe that alone was what he found so appealing. She was different. A novelty. But her position as the twins' nanny was just too crucial to put in jeopardy.

Maybe hiring such an attractive woman had been a bad idea, even if she was the most qualified. Maybe he should have held out and interviewed a few more people, made an effort to find someone older or, better yet, a guy.

"Did you want something?" she asked, and he realized that he was just standing there staring at her.

Way to make yourself look like an idiot, Coop. He was usually pretty smooth when it came to women. He had no idea why he was acting like such a dope.

"I hope I didn't wake you," he said.

"No, I was still up."

"I just wanted to check in, see how it went today."

"It went really well. It'll take some time to get into a routine, but I'm following their lead."

"I'm sorry I wasn't here to help out."

She looked confused. "I didn't expect you to help."

He felt his eyes drifting lower, to the cleavage at the neckline of her gown. She wasn't large-busted, but she wasn't what he would consider small, either. She was…average. So why couldn't he seem to look away?

She noticed him noticing but made no move to cover herself. And why should she? It was her room. He was the intruder.

And he was making a complete ass of himself.

"Was there anything else?" she asked.

He forced his gaze back to her face. "I thought we could just talk for a while. We haven't had a chance to go over the girls' schedules. I thought you might have questions."

She looked hesitant, and he thought her answer was going to be no. And could he blame her? He was behaving like a first-rate pervert. But after several seconds, she said, "Okay, I'll be out in just a minute."

She snapped the door closed and he walked to the kitchen, mentally knocking himself in the head. What the hell was wrong with him? He was acting as if he'd never seen an attractive woman before. One of his dining companions that evening had worn a form-fitting dress that was shorter and lower cut than Sierra's nightgown and he hadn't felt even a twinge of interest. He needed to quit eyeballing her, or she was going to think he was some sort of deviant. The last thing he wanted was for her to be uncomfortable in his home.

Coop opened the wine refrigerator and fished out an open bottle of pinot grigio. Unlike his teammates, he preferred a quality wine to beer or liquor. He'd never been one to enjoy getting drunk. Not since his wild days anyway, when he'd taken pretty much anything that gave him a buzz because at the time it meant taking his pain away.

He took two glasses from the cupboard

and set them on the island countertop. Sierra walked in as he was pouring. She had changed into a pair of black leggings and an oversize, faded yellow T-shirt. He found his gaze drawn to her legs again. He typically dated women who were supermodel skinny—and a few of those women had actually been supermodels— but not necessarily because that was what he preferred. That just seemed to be the type of woman who gravitated toward him. He liked that Sierra had some meat on her bones. She was not heavy by any stretch of the imagination. She just looked…healthy. Although he was sure that most women would take that as an insult.

He quickly reminded himself that it didn't matter what she looked like because she was off-limits.

"Have a seat," he said, and she slid onto one of the bar stools across the island from him. He corked the wine and slid one of the glasses toward her. "I hope you like white."

"Oh…um…" She hesitated, a frown causing

an adorable little wrinkle between her brows. "Maybe I shouldn't."

He put the bottle back in the fridge. Maybe she thought he was trying to get her drunk so he could take advantage of her. "One glass," he said. "Unless you don't drink."

"No, I do. I'm just not sure if it's a good idea."

"Are you underage?"

She flashed him a cute smile. "You know I'm not. I'm just worried that one of the girls might wake up. In fact, I'd say it's a strong possibility, so I need to stay sharp."

"You think one little glass of wine will impair you?" He folded his arms. "You must be quite the lightweight."

Her chin lifted a notch. "I can hold my own. I just don't want to make a bad impression."

"If you drank an entire bottle, that might worry me, but one glass? Do you think I would offer if I thought it was a bad idea?"

"I guess not."

"Let's put it this way: If the twins were your daughters, and you wanted to wind down after a busy day, would you feel comfortable allow-ing yourself a glass of wine?"

"Yes."

He slid the wine closer. "So, stop worrying about what I think, and enjoy."

She took it.

"A toast, to your first day," he said, clinking his glass against hers.

She sipped, nodded and said, "Nice. I wouldn't have imagined you as the wine-drink-ing type."

"I'm sure there are a lot of things about me that would surprise you." He rested his hip against the edge of the countertop. "But tell me about you."

"I thought we were going to talk about the girls."

"We will, but I'd like to know a little bit about you first."

She sipped again, then set her glass down. "You read my file."

"Yeah, but that was just the basics. I'd like to know more about you as a person. Like, what made you get into nursing?"

"My mom, actually."

"She was a nurse?

"No, she was a homemaker. She got breast cancer when I was a kid. The nurses were so wonderful to her and to me and my dad and sister. Especially when she was in hospice. I decided then, that's what I wanted to do."

"She passed away?"

Sierra nodded. "When I was fourteen."

"That's a tough age for a girl to lose her mother."

"It was harder for my sister, I think. She was only ten."

He circled the counter and sat on the stool beside hers. "Is there a good age to lose a parent? I was twelve when my mom and dad died. It was really rough."

"My sister used to be this sweet, happy-go-lucky kid, but after she got really moody and brooding."

"I was angry," he said. "I went from being a pretty decent kid to the class bully."

"It's not uncommon, in that situation, for a boy to pick on someone smaller and weaker.

It probably gave you a feeling of power in an otherwise powerless situation."

"Except I went after kids who were bigger than me. Because I was so big for my age, that usually meant I was fighting boys who were older than me. And I got the snot kicked out of me a couple of times, but usually I won. And you're right, it did make me feel powerful. I felt like it was the only thing I had any control over."

"My sister never picked on anyone, but she was into drugs for a while. Thankfully she cleaned herself up, but when my dad got sick she just couldn't handle it. When she turned eighteen she took off for L.A. She's an actress, or trying to be. She's done a couple of commercials and a few walk-on parts. Mostly she's a waitress."

"What is it that your dad has?" he asked, hoping he wasn't being too nosy.

"He's in the final stages of Alzheimer's."

"How old is he?"

"Fifty."

Damn. "That's really young for Alzheimer's, isn't it?"

She nodded. "It's rare, but it happens. He started getting symptoms when he was forty-six, and the disease progressed much faster than it would in someone older. They tried every drug out there to slow the progression, but nothing seemed to work. It's not likely he'll live out the year."

"I'm so sorry."

She shrugged, eyes lowered, running her thumb around the rim of her glass. "The truth is, he died months ago, at least in all the ways that matter. He's just a shell. A functioning body. I know he hates living this way."

She looked so sad. He wanted to hug her, or rub her shoulder, or do something to comfort her, but it didn't seem appropriate to be touching her. So his only choice was to comfort her with words and shared experiences. Because when it came to losing a parent, he knew just how deeply painful and traumatic it could be.

"When my parents got in the car accident, my dad died instantly. My mom survived the crash, but she was in a coma and brain-dead. My brother, Ash, was eighteen, and he had to make the decision to take her off life support."

"What a horrible thing for him to have to go through. No one should have to make that decision. Not at any age."

"I was too young to really grasp what was happening. I thought he did it because he was mad at her or didn't love her. Only when I got older did I understand that there was no hope."

"I signed a Do Not Resuscitate order for my dad. It was so hard, but I know it's what he wants. Working in the NICU, I've seen parents have to make impossible choices. It was heartbreaking. You have to hold it together at work, be strong for the parents, but I can't tell you how many times I went home and cried my eyes out. Parents of healthy kids just don't realize how lucky they are."

"I can understand how you would burn out in a job like that."

"Don't get me wrong, I really love nursing. I liked that I was helping people. But it can be emotionally draining."

"Do you think you'll miss it?"

She smiled. "With the twins to take care of, I doubt I'll have time."

He hoped she wouldn't eventually burn out, the way she had with nursing. Maybe giving her so little time off had been a bad idea. He knew firsthand how tough it was caring for the twins nonstop. A few hours off on a Sunday and one weekend a month weren't much time. Maybe he should have considered hiring two nannies, one for during the week, and one for the weekends. "You're sure it's not going to be too much?"

"Watching the twins?"

"By taking this job, you're pretty much giving up your social life."

"I gave that up when my dad got too sick to care for himself. He couldn't be alone, so we had a caregiver while I worked, then I took over when I got home."

"Every day? That sounds expensive."

She nodded. "It was. We blew through his savings in just a few months. But I didn't want him to have to go in a nursing home. I kept him with me as long as I could. But eventually it got to the point where I just couldn't provide the best care for him."

"When did you go out? Have fun?"

"I've always been more of a homebody."

"What about dating?"

The sudden tuck between her brows said her love life was a touchy subject. And really it was none of his business. Or maybe she thought it was some sort of cheesy pickup line.

"You can tell me to mind my own business," he said.

"It's okay. Things are just a little complicated right now. I'm not in a good place emotionally to be getting into a relationship." She glanced over at him. "That's probably tough for someone like you to understand."

"Someone so morally vacant?"

Her eyes widened. "No, I didn't mean—"

"It's okay," he said with a laugh. "A few weeks ago, I probably wouldn't have understood."

Dating and being out with other people had been such an intrinsic part of who he was, he probably wouldn't have been able to grasp the concept of leading a quiet, domesticated life. Since the crash that had taken his brother, his attitude and his perception about what was really important had been altered. Like tonight for instance. Why go out barhopping to meet a woman for what would ultimately be a meaningless and quite frankly unsatisfying encounter when the twins needed him at home?

"Priorities change," he said.

She nodded. "Yes they do. You see things a certain way, then suddenly it's not about what you want anymore."

He wondered if she was talking about her dad. "I know exactly what you mean."

"You really love them," she said.

"The twins?" he found himself grinning. "Yeah, I do. What's not to love? This was obviously not a part of my plans, but I want to do right by them. I owe Ash that much. He sacrificed a lot to raise me. He worked two jobs and put college off for years to be there for me, and believe me, I was a handful. Some people thought that because the twins aren't Ash's biological kids it somehow absolved me of all responsibility. Even their birth mother seemed to think so."

"What do you mean?"

"Her lawyer contacted my lawyer. Apparently she saw on the news that Ash and Susan had died and she wanted the girls back. I can only assume that she thought I would be a failure as a dad."

"And you didn't consider it?"

"Not for a second. And even if I didn't think I could handle taking care of the girls myself, why would I give them to someone who didn't want them to begin with?"

That tuck was back between her brows. "Maybe she wanted them but just couldn't keep them. Maybe she thought giving them up was the best thing for the twins."

"And that changed in five months? She thinks she can give the girls more than I can? With me they'll never want for a thing. They'll have the best of everything. Clothes, education, you name it. Could she do that?"

"So you assume that because she isn't rich

she wouldn't be a good parent?" she asked in a sharp tone.

For someone who didn't even know the birth mother she was acting awfully defensive. "The truth is, I don't know why she gave them up, but it doesn't matter. My brother adopted the twins and loved them like his own flesh and blood. He wanted the girls raised by me, and I'm honoring his wishes."

Her expression softened. "I'm sorry, I didn't mean to snap. In my line of work, I've seen young mothers harshly misjudged. It's a natural instinct to defend them."

"Not to mention that you've no doubt heard about my reputation and question my ability to properly raise the girls."

She shook her head. "I didn't say—"

"You didn't have to." It was amazing the people who had strong opinions about his ability to be a good father. Some of his closest friends— the single ones—thought he was crazy for taking on the responsibility. And the friends with families—not that he had many of those— openly doubted his capabilities as a parent.

He intended to prove them all wrong.

"Like I said before," he told Sierra firmly, meaning every word, "priorities change. For me, the girls come first, and they always will."

Four

Sierra could hardly believe how snippy she had gotten with Coop last night.

She replayed the conversation in her head as she got the girls ready for their afternoon nap, cringing inwardly as she placed Ivy on her belly on the carpet with a toy while she wrestled a wiggling Fern out of her jumper and into a fresh diaper.

Antagonize your boss. Way to go Sierra. Was she *trying* to get fired? Or even worse, give him any reason to doubt that she was just the twin's nanny? But all that garbage about him changing his priorities had really ruffled her feathers, and she didn't believe it for a minute, not after the way he was ogling her when she opened the bedroom door in her nightgown. And if he thought she would be interested in a man like him, he was dreaming.

Although she couldn't deny that in a very small and completely depraved way it had been just the tiniest bit exciting. And to his credit Coop had looked conflicted, like he knew it was wrong, but he just couldn't help himself. Which she was sure summed him up in a nutshell. He would try to change, try to be a good father to the twins, but in the end he would fail because that was just the sort of man he was.

But it had been an awfully long time since someone had looked at her in a sexual way, and what woman wouldn't feel at least the tiniest bit special to be noticed by a rich, gorgeous guy who was known for dating actresses and supermodels? She also didn't let herself forget that he was a womanizer, and she was one of hundreds of women he had looked at in that very same way.

She laid Fern in her crib and turned to pick

up Ivy, but she had rolled all the way across the room and wound up by the closet door.

"Come back here, you little sneak," she said, scooping her up and nibbling the ticklish spot on her neck. Ivy giggled and squirmed, but when Sierra laid her on the changing table she didn't put up a fuss. She was definitely the milder mannered of the two, but she had a curious nature. Sierra was sure that left to her own devices, Ivy could get herself into trouble. There was no doubt that Ivy was more like her, and Fern seemed to take after their birth father's side of the family. Sierra was having such a blast getting to know them, learning all their little personality quirks. She realized how fortunate she was to have this opportunity and she wouldn't take it for granted. And if being with her daughters meant putting up with an occasional inappropriate glance, it was worth it.

Speaking of Mr. Inappropriate, Sierra heard the deep timbre of Coop's voice from his office down the hall. He was on the phone again. He was working from home today, or so he said.

Exactly what he was doing in there, or what that so-called "work" entailed, she wasn't sure. Polishing his various trophies? Giving interviews?

Other than basking in the glow of his former fame, she wasn't sure what he did with his time.

She laid Ivy in her crib and blew each of the girls a kiss good-night, then she closed the curtain to smother the light and stepped out of the room...colliding with Coop, who was on his way in. He said, "Whoa!" looking just as surprised to see her as she was to see him. She instinctively held her hands up to soften the inevitable collision and wound up with her palms pressed against the hard wall of his chest, breathing in the warm and clean aroma of his skin. He wore the scent of soap and shampoo the way other men wore three-hundred dollar cologne. And though it was completely irrational, the urge to slide her hands up around his neck, to plaster herself against him, hit her swift and hard.

Touching Coop was clearly a bad idea.

She pulled away so fast her upper back and head hit the door frame with a thud.

Coop winced. "You okay?"

She grimaced and rubbed her head. "Fine."

"You sure? You hit that pretty hard." He reached behind her and cupped the back of her head in one enormous palm, but his touch was gentle as he probed for an injury, his fingers slipping through her hair beneath the root of her ponytail, spreading warmth against her scalp. "I don't feel a bump."

But, oh man, did it feel nice.

Nice? Ugh! This was insane. Knowing the sort of man he was, his touch should have repulsed her.

She ducked away from his hand. "I'm fine, really. You just startled me."

He frowned, tucking his hands in the pockets of his jeans, as if maybe he realized that touching her wasn't appropriate. Or maybe he liked it as much as she did. "Sorry. Where are the girls?"

"I just put them down for their nap."

"Why didn't you tell me? I'd like to say good-night."

Honestly, she hadn't thought it would matter to him. "I thought I heard you on the phone and I didn't want to disturb you."

"Well, next time let me know," he said, sounding irritated. "If I'm here, the girls come first."

"Okay. I'm sorry. They're still awake if you want to see them."

His expression softened. "Just for a second."

He disappeared into their room and Sierra walked to the kitchen to clean up the girls' lunch dishes. Coop really was taking this "being there for the girls" business pretty seriously. But how long would that last? It was probably a novelty, being the caring uncle. She was sure it wouldn't be long before he slipped back into his old ways and wouldn't have the time or the inclination to say good-night to the twins.

"What is this?" Ms. Densmore snipped, holding up the empty bottles from the girls' lunch as Sierra walked into the kitchen.

Was this some sort of trick question? "Um… bottles?"

She flung daggers with her eyes. "And why were they on the kitchen counter and not in the dishwasher?"

"Because I didn't put them there yet."

"Anything you use in the kitchen must be put in the dishwasher or washed by *you*. And any messes you and the children make are yours to clean."

"I'm aware of that," Sierra said, and only because Ms. Densmore had given her this identical lecture *three* times now. "I planned to clean up after I put the twins down for their nap. Their *care* is my priority."

"I also noticed a basket of your clothes in the laundry room. I'd like to remind you that you are responsible for your own laundry. That includes clothing, towels and bedding. I work for Mr. Landon. Not you or anyone else. Is that clear?"

Sienna gritted her teeth. She was sure it bugged the hell out of the housekeeper that she was forced to feed Sierra, although Coop was right about her being an excellent cook. "The washer was already running so I set them there temporarily."

Sierra had done absolutely nothing to offend her, so she had no clue why Ms. Densmore was so cranky, so inclined to dislike her.

"As I have said to Mr. Landon on numerous occasions, I took this job because there were no children. I am not a nanny or a babysitter. Do not ask me to hold, change, feed or play with the twins. They are *your* responsibility, and yours alone."

As if she'd want her girls anywhere near this nasty old bitch. "I'm pretty clear on that, thanks."

Ms. Densmore shoved the bottles at her and Sierra took them. Then, her pointy, beak nose in the air, Ms. Densmore stalked away to the laundry room behind the kitchen. And though it was petty and immature, Sierra gestured rudely to her retreating back.

"That wasn't very ladylike."

She spun around to find Coop watching her, a wry grin on his face.

He folded his arms across his ridiculously wide chest and said, "I'm glad the girls weren't here to see that."

She bit her lip and hooked her hands behind her back. "Um…sorry?"

Coop laughed. "I'm kidding. I would have done exactly the same thing. And you're right, the girls are your first priority. The dishwasher can wait."

"I have no idea why she dislikes me so much."

"Don't take it personally. She doesn't like me, either, but she's one hell of an awesome housekeeper."

"You would think she would be happy to have me here. Now she doesn't have to deal with the twins."

"I'll have a talk with her."

That could be a really bad idea. "Maybe you shouldn't. I don't want her to think I tattled on her. It will just make things worse."

"Don't worry, I'll take care of it."

Coop walked to the laundry room and over the sound of the washer and dryer she heard the door snap closed behind him. Tempted as she was to sneak back there and press her ear to the door to listen, she put the lunch dishes in the dishwasher instead. Coop was back a couple of minutes later, a satisfied smile on his face.

"She won't hassle you anymore," he said. "If you need me, I'll be in my office."

Whatever he'd said to Ms. Densmore, it had worked. She came out of the laundry room several minutes later, red faced with either embarrassment or anger, and didn't say a word or even look at Sierra. She maintained her tight-lipped silence until dinnertime when she served a Mexican dish that was so delicious Sierra had two helpings.

Sierra was surprised when Coop invited her to eat in the dining room with him. She had just assumed that she would be treated like any other hired help and eat in the kitchen with the girls. Because surely he wouldn't want two infants around making a fuss and disrupting his meal. But he actually insisted on it. While Sierra sat at one end of the table, Ivy in her high chair next to her, he sat with Fern, alternately feeding her then himself. When Fern started to fuss and Sierra offered to take over, he refused. He wiped applesauce from her face and hands with a washcloth, plucked her from her high chair and sat her in his lap while he finished his meal, dodging her grasping hands as she tried to intercept his fork. After their talk last night, maybe he felt he had to prove some sort of point.

When they were done with dinner he switched on the enormous flat-screen television in the living room and tuned it to ESPN. Then he stretched out on the floor and played with the girls while she sat on the couch feeling a little like an outsider.

The girls obviously adored him and it scared the hell out of her. Not because she thought they would love him more. She'd reconciled her position in the girls' lives. She just hated to see the girls become attached to him, only to have him grow bored with parenting. They were a novelty, but his fascination with them would fade. He was still reeling from his brother's death, but that would only last so long. Eventually he would go back to his womanizing, partying ways. And when he did, *she* would be there to offer the stability they needed. She was the person the twins would learn to depend on.

The worst part was that he had flat-out admitted he thought that he could buy their affection by giving them "the best money could buy," but what they really needed, his love and emotional support, he wasn't capable of giving. Not for any extended length of time.

When it was time for the twins to go to bed Coop helped her wrestle them into their pajamas. He gave them each a kiss good-night, then he and Sierra laid them in their cribs.

On their way out of the room Sierra grabbed their soiled clothes from the day and switched off the light. "I'm going to go throw these in the wash."

"You don't have to do the girls' laundry," Coop said, following her down the hall. "Leave it for Ms. Densmore."

"It's okay. I wanted to do a few of my own things, too. Unless you'd prefer I wash the twins' clothes separately."

He looked confused. "Why would I care about that?"

Sierra shrugged. "Some people are picky about the way their kids' clothes are washed."

"Well, not me."

Somehow she didn't imagine he would be. And he probably wouldn't care that she had every intention of washing their "hand wash only" dresses on Delicate in the machine.

Sierra dumped the clothes in the washing machine, noting that the room was tidy to point of fanaticism. There wasn't so much as a speck of dust on the floor or a stitch of clothing any-where. Ms. Densmore must have been as anal about keeping the laundry done as she was with keeping the house clean.

Sierra opened the cabinet to find the deter-gents, stain removers and fabric softeners orga-nized neatly by function and perfectly aligned so the labels were facing out. She grabbed the liquid detergent, measured out a cupful and poured it into the machine. She put the cap back on, ignoring the small bit that sloshed over the side of the bottle, then, smiling serenely, stuck it back on the shelf crooked. She did the same with the fabric softener, then gave the stain removers a quick jostle just for fun before she started the machine.

She walked back out into the kitchen and found Coop sitting at the island on a barstool, two glasses of red wine on the counter.

"Take a load off," he said, nudging the other stool with his foot. "I was in the mood for red tonight. It's a Malbec. I hope that's okay."

She wasn't picky. However, she had just assumed that last night's shared wine had been a one-time thing. "You don't have to serve me wine every night."

"I know I don't."

Did he plan to make a habit of this because she wasn't sure if she was comfortable with that. Not that she minded relaxing with a glass of wine at the end of the day. It was the company that made her a little nervous. Especially when he sat so darned close to her. Last night she'd sat beside him feeling edgy, as if she were waiting for him to pounce. Which he didn't, of course. He had been a perfect gentleman. Yet he still made her nervous.

"Maybe we could sit in the living room," she suggested. Far, far away from each other.

Coop shrugged. "Sure."

What she would rather do is take the glass to her room and curl up in bed with the mystery novel she'd been reading, but she didn't want to be rude.

He sprawled in the chair by the window, his long, muscular legs stretched out in front of him, and Sierra sat with her legs tucked underneath her on the corner of the couch. He was yards away from her, so why the tension lingering in the air? And why could she not stop looking at him? Yes, he was easy on the eyes, but she didn't even like him.

Coop sipped his wine, then rested the glass on his stomach—which was no doubt totally ripped and as perfect as the rest of him—his fingers laced together and cupping the bowl. "What do you think of the wine?"

She took a sip, letting it roll around her tongue. She didn't know much about wines, but it tasted pretty good to her. Very bold and fruity. A huge step up from the cheap brands she could afford. "I like it. It tastes expensive."

"It is. But what's the point of having all this money if I can't enjoy the finer things? Which reminds me, I talked to my decorator today. He's tied up with another project and won't be available to meet with you for at least three weeks. If that's not soon enough for you, we can find someone who's available now."

"Three weeks is fine. There's no rush."

"You're sure?"

"Positive. I really appreciate that you want me to be comfortable, though." The truth was, she hadn't been spending much time in there anyway. The twins kept her busy all day, and when she was in her room, she was usually asleep.

"I meant to ask you yesterday—what's going on with your dad? You mentioned moving him to a different place."

"They're taking him by ambulance to the new nursing home Saturday morning."

"Do you need to be there?"

Even if she did, she had a responsibility to the girls. "He's in good hands. I'll be visiting him Sunday during my time off. I can get him settled in then."

"You know, you don't have to wait until Sundays to see him. You can go anytime you'd like. I don't mind if you take the girls with you."

"He's going to be all the way out in Jersey. I don't own a car and taking the twins on the train or the bus would be a logistical nightmare."

He shrugged. "So take my car."

"I can't."

"It's okay, really."

"No, I mean I *really* can't. I don't know how."

His brows rose. "You never learned to drive?"

"I've always lived in the city. I never needed to. And gas prices being what they are, public transportation just makes more sense."

"Well then, why don't I take you? We could go Saturday when he's transferred."

Huh? Why would he want to take time out of his day to haul her to Jersey? Surely he had something better to do. "You really don't have to do that."

"I want to."

She didn't know what to say. Why was he being so nice to her? Why did he even care if she saw her dad? He was her employer, not her pal.

"You're looking at me really weirdly right now," Coop said. "Either you're not used to people doing nice things for you, or you're seriously questioning my motives."

A little bit of both actually, and it was creepy how he seemed to always know what she was thinking. "I'm sure you have other things—"

"No, I don't. My schedule is totally free this weekend." He paused, then added, "And for the record, I have no ulterior motives."

She had a hard time buying that. "You're sure it's no trouble?"

"None at all. And I'll bet the girls would like to get out of the house."

Sierra was going to remind him that she'd taken them for a long walk in the park that morning, but it seemed like a moot point. He obviously wasn't going to take no for an answer, and she really would like to be there when they moved her dad, not only to make certain he was handled respectfully, but also to see that none of his very few possessions were left behind. The pictures and keepsakes. Not that he would know either way. Maybe, she thought sadly, it would be best if she just held on to them now.

"I'll call the nursing home tomorrow and find out when the ambulance will be there. Maybe we could be there a half an hour or so beforehand, then follow them over to the new facility."

"Just let me know when and I'll be ready."

"Thanks."

He narrowed his eyes slightly. "But…you're still wondering why I'm doing this for you. You apparently have this preconceived notion about the kind of person that I am."

She couldn't deny it. He would be surprised by how much she actually did know about him. The real stuff, not the rumors and conjecture. But she couldn't tell him that.

"Believe it or not, I'm a pretty decent guy." He paused then added, "And an above-average dancer."

She would have to take his word on that. "I clearly have trust issues," she said. Fool me once, shame on you, and all of that. Maybe he didn't have ulterior motives, but that was not usually the case. And under normal circumstances she would have told him no on principle alone, but just this one time she would make an exception.

"I guess it will just take time for you to believe that I'm not a bad guy," he said.

Honestly, she didn't understand why he cared what she thought of him. Was he this personable with all of his employees? Granted she had only worked for him a couple of days, but she had never seen him offer Ms. Densmore a glass of wine or heard him offer to drive her anywhere. She was sure it had a lot to do with Sierra being young and, yes, she was what most men considered attractive. Not a raving beauty but not too shabby, either. Then again, she was nowhere near as glamorous as the women she had seen him linked to in the past. But Coop hadn't been born wealthy. Who was to say he didn't enjoy slumming it occasionally?

Well, if he thought doing nice things for her was a direct route into her pants, that just because he was rich and famous and above average in the looks department she would go all gooey, he was in for a rude awakening.

Five

Sierra stood in her dad's new room, resisting the natural instinct to step in and help as the ambulance attendants worked with the nursing home staff to get her dad moved from the gurney to his bed, where he would most likely spend the rest of his life. At least in this new facility the staff was friendly and helpful and she could rest easy knowing that her dad would be well cared for. Unfortunately the ambulance had been an hour late to pick him up and the paperwork had taken an eternity.

Coop had been incredibly patient, taking over with the twins, but that patience had to be wearing thin by now. He was sitting in the rec room with them, and though she had fed them their lunch in the car on the way over, they were about an hour and a half past their nap time and last time she checked were getting fussy. She was thankful to have been around for the transfer, but she felt the crushing weight of guilt for making Coop—her employer—wait around for her.

She would have to make this visit a short one.

Once they got him situated in bed, everyone cleared out of the room. The nurse must have mistaken her guilt for conflicted feelings about her dad because she rubbed Sierra's arm, smiled warmly and said, "Don't worry, honey, we'll take good care of him."

When she was gone Sierra walked over to the bed. The curtain between him and his roommate was drawn, but according to the nurse, the man in the next bed was also comatose. "I can't stay, Dad, but I'll come back tomorrow, I promise."

She kissed his cheek, feeling guilty for cutting her visit so short, and headed to the rec room where Coop and the girls were waiting for her. To look at him, no one would guess that he was a multi-millionaire celebrity. In jeans, a T-shirt and worn tennis shoes, pacing the floor, looking completely at ease with one restless twin in each arm, he looked like just a regular guy. Albeit most "regular" guys weren't six-three with the physique of an Adonis.

She would be lying if she denied it was an adorable sight, the way he bounced the girls patiently. For someone who hadn't anticipated being a dad, and had the duty thrust on him unexpectedly, he had done amazingly well. She couldn't help but wonder if she had been unfairly harsh on him. In the five days she'd worked for him she had seen no hint of the womanizing party animal. So why couldn't she shake the feeling that he was destined to let the girls down?

It was all very confusing.

"I'm so sorry it's taken this long," she told him, plucking a wiggling Ivy from him.

"It's okay," Coop said, looking as though he genuinely meant it. "Is he all settled in?"

"Finally." Ivy squirmed in her arms, so Sierra transferred her to the opposite hip. "Let's get out of here. These two are way past their nap time."

"You don't want to stay and visit a little longer?"

She figured by now he would have been exasperated with the girls' fussing and would be gunning to get back on the road for home. To his credit, though, he hadn't once complained. Not while they sat at the other nursing home waiting for the transport, or when they sat stuck in weekend traffic. But as much as she would love to stay for just a little while longer, to make sure the trip had no adverse effects on her dad physically, she had already taken up way too much of Coop's personal time.

"I'll come by tomorrow on my time off," she told Coop, grabbing the packed-to-the-gills designer label diaper bag and slinging it over her shoulder. Coop commandeered the double umbrella stroller—top-of-the-line, of course, because when it came to the twins Ash and Susan had spared no expense—and they walked out of the building and through the parking lot to his vehicle. Earlier that morning, as she waited on the sidewalk outside his building for him to bring the car around, she'd expected either some flashy little sports car—which logistically she knew wouldn't work with two infants—or at the opposite end of the excess spectrum, a Hummer. Instead he had pulled up in a low-key silver SUV, proving once again that the man she thought she had pegged and the real Cooper were two very different people.

She and Coop each buckled a twin into her car seat, and within five minutes of exiting the lot, both girls were out cold.

"So, where to now?" Coop asked.

Sierra just assumed they would head back into the city. "Home, I guess."

"But it's a gorgeous summer afternoon. We should do something. I don't know about you, but I'm starving. Why don't we grab a bite to eat?"

"The girls just fell asleep. If we wake them up now and drag them into a restaurant, I don't anticipate it being a pleasant experience."

"Good point."

"Besides, don't you need to get home? It's Saturday. You must have plans for later."

"Nope, no plans tonight," Coop said.

He hadn't gone out the night before, either. The four of them had eaten dinner together, then Coop wrestled and played with the twins until their bedtime. After they were tucked into bed, Sierra thought for sure that he would go out, but when she emerged from the laundry room after putting in her daily load of soiled clothes, Coop had been sitting in the living room with two glasses of wine. And though she had planned on reading for a while then going to sleep early, it seemed rude to turn him down after he had gone through the trouble of actually pouring the wine.

One quick glass, she had promised herself, and she would be in bed before nine-thirty. But one glass turned into two, and she and Coop got to talking about his hockey playing days—a subject that even she had to admit was pretty interesting—and before she knew it, it was nearly midnight. Though he did still make her a little nervous and the idea of a friendship with him made her slightly uncomfortable, he was so easygoing and charming she couldn't help but like him.

"On our way in we passed a deli and a small park," he said. "We could pick up sandwiches, eat in the car, then go for a drive while the twins sleep."

That actually wasn't a bad idea. If they took the twins home now, the minute they took them out of their car seats they would probably wake up, cutting their nap short by at least an hour, which would probably make them crabby for the rest of the day. But the idea of spending so much time in such close quarters with Coop made her nervous. Not that she was worried he would act inappropriately. If he had wanted to try something, he would have done it by now, and aside from ogling her in her nightie the other evening—which admittedly was her own fault for not putting on a robe—he'd been a perfect gentleman. These feelings of unease were her own doing.

Illogical and inappropriate as it was, she

was attracted to Coop, and clearly the feeling was mutual. The air felt electrically charged whenever he was near, and then there was that unwelcome little zap of energy that passed between them whenever they touched, even if it was something as innocent as their fingers brushing when he handed her a jar of baby food. And even though she had no intention whatsoever of expanding the dynamics of their relationship to include intimacy, she couldn't shake the feeling that they were crossing some line of morality.

But what the heck, it was just a sandwich. And it really was the best thing for the girls, and that was what mattered, right?

"I could eat," she said.

"Great." He flashed her one of those adorable grins. The dimpled kind that made her heart go all wonky.

God, she was pathetic.

Though she offered to go inside the deli and order the food while he waited with the girls, he insisted on going himself and refused the money she tried to give him to cover the expense of her food.

"You shouldn't have to pay for my lunch," she told him.

"If we were at home you would be eating food that I paid for, so what's the difference?"

It was tough to argue with logic like that. Besides, he was out of the car before she could utter another word.

He was in and back out of the deli in five minutes with his grilled Reuben and her turkey on whole grain. He also got coleslaw, a bag of potato chips, bottled water and sodas. They found the park a few blocks away and parked in a spot facing the playground under the shade of a tree. Sierra worried the girls might wake up when he shut the engine off, but they were both out cold.

They spread their lunch out on the console and started eating.

"Can I ask you a question?" she said.

"Sure."

"Besides being a celebrity, what do you do now? For a living, I mean. Do you work?"

Her question seemed to amuse him. "I work really hard actually. I have my own line of hockey equipment coming out, and I started a chain of sports centers a few years ago and they've taken off. We're opening six more by next January."

"What kind of sports centers?"

"Ice rinks and indoor playing fields. Kids sports are big business these days. On top of that I own a couple dozen vacation properties around the world that I rent out. Also very lucrative."

Wow, so much for her theory that he sat around basking in his former fame. It sounded as if he kept himself really busy.

"Where are the vacation homes?" she asked him.

He named off the different cities, and then described the sorts of properties he owned. The list was an impressive one. Clearly he was a very sharp businessman.

"I never realized there was such a market for rental vacation homes."

"Most people aren't in a financial position to

drop the money on a home they may only use a couple of times a year, so they rent. Not only is it a lot cheaper, but also you're not locked into one city or country."

She reached into the bag of chips for her third handful.

"I guess you were hungry," Coop teased.

She shot him a look. "Be careful, or you'll give me a complex."

"Are you kidding? I think it's great that you eat like a normal human being. I've taken women to some of the finest restaurants in the city and they order a side salad and seltzer water, or, even worse, they order a huge expensive meal and eat three bites."

"Maybe this is a dumb question, but if it bothers you so much, why do you always date super-skinny women? I mean, doesn't that sort of come with the territory?"

"Convenience, I guess."

Her brows rose. *"Convenience?"*

"They just happen to be the kind of women who hang around the people I hang around with."

"You mean, the kind who throw themselves at you."

He shrugged. "More or less."

"Have you ever had to actually pursue a woman you wanted to date?"

He thought about that for a second, then shook his head and said, "No, not really. In fact, never."

"Seriously? Not once? Not even in high school?"

"Since I was old enough to take an interest in girls I was the team star. Girls flocked to me."

She shook her head in disbelief. "Wow. That's just...*wow.*"

"Can you blame them? I mean, look at me. I'm rich, good-looking, a famous athlete. Who wouldn't want me? I'm completely irresistible."

She couldn't tell if he was serious or just teasing her. Could he honestly be *that* arrogant? "I wouldn't."

That seemed to amuse him. "You already do. You try to pretend you don't, but I can sense it."

"I think you've been hit in the head with a hockey stick a few too many times because I do *not* want you. You aren't even my type."

"But that's what makes it so exciting. You know you shouldn't like me, you know it's wrong because you work for me, but you just can't stop thinking about me."

How did he do that? How did he always seem to know what was going on inside her head? It was probably the third or fourth time he'd done this to her. It couldn't just be a lucky guess.

It was disturbing and…fascinating. And no way in *hell* could she ever let him know just how right he was. "So what you're saying is, all that stuff about you being a nice guy was bull. Everything nice that you've done is because you've been trying to get into my pants?"

"No, I am a nice guy. And for the record, if all I wanted was to get into your pants, I'd have been there by now."

Her eyes went wide. "Oh, really?"

"You're not nearly as tough as you think you are. If I tried to kiss you right now, you wouldn't stop me."

The thought of him leaning over the console and pressing his lips to hers made her heart flutter and her stomach bottom out. But she squared her shoulders and said, "If you tried to kiss me, you would be wearing the family jewels for earrings."

He threw his head back and laughed.

"You don't think I would do it?"

"No, you probably would, just to prove how tough you are. Then you would give in and let me kiss you anyway."

"The depth of your arrogance is truly re-markable."

"It's one of my most charming qualities," he said, but his grin said that he was definitely teasing her this time.

Maybe the confidence was a smoke screen, or this was his way of testing the waters or teas-ing her. Maybe he really liked her, but being so used to women throwing themselves at him, the possibility of being rejected scared him.

Weirdly enough, the idea that under the tough-guy exterior there could be a vulnera-ble man made him that much more appealing.

Ugh. What was *wrong* with her?

"Even if I did want you," she said, "which,

despite what you believe, I really don't, I would never risk it. I can't even imagine putting my father back in that hellhole we just got him out of. And without this job I can't even come close to affording the new place. So I have every reason *not* to want you."

Before Coop had time to process that, Ivy began to stir in the backseat.

"Uh-oh," he said, glancing back at her. "We better get moving before she wakes up."

He balled up the paper wrapper from his sandwich and shoved it back in the bag, then started the engine. She thought once they got moving, he might segue back into the conversation, but he turned the radio on instead, and she breathed a silent sigh of relief. She hoped she had made her point, he would drop the subject forever and the sexual tension that had been a constant companion in their relationship would magically disappear. Then they could have a normal employee/employer relationship. Because she feared Coop was right. If he kissed her, she wasn't sure she would be able to tell him no.

And she had the sinking feeling that this conversation, inappropriate as it was, was nowhere close to over.

Six

Sierra didn't hear from her sister very often. She would go months at a time without a single word. Sierra would call and leave messages that Joy wouldn't return, send cards that would come back as undeliverable. Then out of the blue Joy would call and always with the same feeble excuses. She was crazy-busy, or had moved, or her phone had been disconnected because she couldn't pay the bill. But the reality was that Joy was fragile. Watching their mother slowly waste away had damaged her. She simply didn't have the emotional capacity to handle the hopelessness of their dad's illness and dealt with it by moving a couple thousand miles away and cutting off all contact.

Sierra hadn't even been able to reach her when she learned about Ash and Susan's death, and frankly she could have used a bit of emotional support. Which was why Sierra was surprised to see her name on her caller ID that night after she and Coop put the twins to bed. She had just stepped out of the room and was closing the door when her phone started to ring.

She considered not answering, giving Joy a taste of her own medicine for a change. Sometimes she got tired of being the responsible sister. But after two rings guilt got the best of her. Suppose it was something important? And what if Joy didn't call again for months? Besides their dad and the twins, Sierra had no one else. Not to mention that it was an awesome excuse to skip the post-bedtime glass of wine with Coop. And after what had happened this afternoon, the less time she spent with him the better.

"It's my sister. I have to take this," she said, slipping into her bedroom and shutting the door, pretending she didn't see the brief flash of disappointment that passed across his face.

"Guess who!" Joy chirped when Sierra answered.

"Hey, sis." She sat on the edge of her bed. "What's it been, three months?"

That earned a long-suffering sigh from her sister. "I know, I know, I should call more often. But what I've got to say now will make up for it."

"Oh, yeah?" Somehow she doubted that.

"I'm coming home!"

"You're moving back to New York?"

Sierra's heart lifted, then swiftly plunged when her sister laughed and said, "God, no! Are you kidding? Los Angeles is too fabulous to leave. I'm staying at a friend's Malibu beachfront home and it's totally amazing. In fact, I'm sitting in the sand, watching the tide move in as we speak."

She could just picture Joy in one of her flowing peasant skirts and gauzy blouses, her long, tanned legs folded beneath her, her waist-length, wavy black hair blowing in the salty breeze. She would be holding a designer beer in her hand with one of those skinny cigarettes she liked to smoke dangling between two fingers. She had always been so much cooler than Sierra, so much more self-confident. Yet so tortured. And she was sure that the friend Joy was staying with was a man and that she was also sharing his bedroom.

"Then why did you say you're coming home?" Sierra asked.

"Because I'm flying in for a visit."

"When?"

"A week from this coming Wednesday. They're holding auditions for an independent film that's supposed to start filming this August and my agent thinks I'm a shoo-in for the lead roll. I'll be in town a week just in case I get a callback."

"That sounds promising." Although according to Joy, her agent thought she was a shoo-in for every role he set her up for, or so it seemed.

"I know what you're thinking," Joy said.

"I didn't say a word."

"You didn't have to. I can feel your skepticism over the phone line. But this is different. My new agent has some really awesome connections."

"New agent? What happened to the old one?"

"I didn't tell you about that? We parted ways about two months ago."

And Sierra hadn't talked to her in three months. "Why? I thought he was some sort of super-agent."

"His wife sort of caught us going at it in his office."

"You *slept* with your *married* agent?" Why did that not surprise her?

"A girl does what she can to get ahead, and it was no hardship, believe me. Besides, you're not exactly in a position to pass judgment."

Technically the twins' father was a married man, but it was a totally different situation. "He and his wife were separated, and it was only that one night."

By the time she realized she was pregnant, he and his wife had reconciled. Not that she would have wanted to marry him. He was a nice guy, but they both knew right after it happened that it had been a mistake.

"So, you said you're coming to visit?" Sierra said, changing the subject.

"For a week. And needless to say, I'll be staying with my favorite sister."

"Oh." That was going to be a problem.

"What do you mean, 'oh'? I thought you would be happy to see me."

"I am. It's just that staying with me is going to be a problem."

"Why? Don't tell me you're living with someone. And even if you are, he damned well better let your baby sister stay for a couple of nights."

"I actually am living with someone, but not in the way that you think. I mean, we're not a couple. I work for him."

"As a nurse?"

"As a nanny."

"A *nanny?* You gave the girls up, what, six months ago? Isn't that, like, a painful reminder?"

"Joy, hold on a minute, I have to check something." She walked to her door and opened it a crack. If she was going to tell Joy what was going on, she didn't want to risk Coop over-hearing. From the living room she could hear the television and knew he was probably in his favorite chair, engrossed in whatever sporting event he was watching. She closed her door and walked back to the bed. "Did you get any of my messages about the twins' adoptive parents?"

"I did, yeah. I wanted to call, but...you know..."

She was sorry, but she couldn't deal with it. Same old story. "Well, the girls went to their uncle, Ash's brother."

"Isn't he like some famous athlete or some-thing?"

"A former hockey player. A womanizing party animal. Not exactly the sort of person I wanted raising my girls."

"Oh, Si, I'm so sorry. Have you talked to your lawyer? Is there anything he can do? Can you claim he's unfit and get the girls back?"

She fidgeted with the edge of the pillowcase, knowing this next part was not going to go over well. "My lawyer talked to his lawyer, but he refused to give them up. There's nothing I can do. So I took matters into my own hands."

Joy gasped. "You *kidnapped* them?"

Sierra laughed. "Of course not! I would never do something like that. But I needed to be there for them, to know that they were okay, so when I heard that he was looking for a nanny…"

Another gasp. "Are you saying that *you're* the twins' nanny?"

"You should see them, Joy. They're so beautiful and so sweet. And I get to be with them 24/7."

"And this guy, their uncle, he knows you're their mother?"

"God, no! And he can never know."

"Sierra, that's *crazy*. What are you going to do, just take care of the girls for the rest of your life, with them never knowing that you're their birth mother?"

"I'll stay with them as long as they need me. And maybe some day I can tell them the truth."

"What about your life? What about men and marriage and having more kids? You're just going to give that all up."

"Not forever. I figure once they're in school full-time they won't need me nearly as much. As long as I'm here in the mornings and when they get home after school, they won't really need me to spend the night."

"It sounds as if you have it all figured out."

"I do."

"And this uncle…"

"Coop. Coop Landon."

"Is he really awful?"

In a way she wished he was. It would make this a lot less confusing. "Actually, he seems like a good guy. So far. Not at all what I expected." Almost too good, *too* nice. "He's really committed to taking care of the twins. For now anyway. That doesn't mean he won't eventually revert back to his old ways. That's why it's so important that I'm here for the girls. To see that they're raised properly."

"Suppose he finds out who you are? What then?"

"He won't. The original birth certificate is sealed, and obviously Ash and Susan never told him. There's no possible way that he could find out."

"Famous last words."

She brushed off her sister's concerns. "Just be happy for me, okay? This is what I want."

"Oh, honey, I am happy for you. I just don't want to see you hurt."

"I won't be. It's foolproof." As long as she didn't do something stupid, like fall for Coop. "So anyway, that's why you can't stay with me. I'm living in his Upper East Side penthouse apartment."

"Sounds…roomy."

Not that roomy. "Joy, you can't stay here."

"Why not? You said this Coop is a good guy. I'm sure he wouldn't mind."

"Joy—"

"You could at least ask. Because frankly I have nowhere else to go. My credit cards are maxed out and I have three dollars in my checking account. My agent had to lend me the money for the ticket, which of course is nonrefundable. If I can't stay with you, I'm crashing on a park bench."

She would pay for a hotel for her sister if she could, but there wasn't a decent place within thirty blocks that was less that one-fifty a night. The expense of moving their dad had taken up all of Sierra's cash, and like Joy, her credit cards were maxed out. It was going to take her months to catch up. And though she hated the idea of taking advantage of Coop's hospitality, this could be the perfect opportunity for a dose of emotional blackmail. "I'll ask him on one condition."

"Anything."

"You have to swear that when you're here you'll come with me to see Dad."

She sighed heavily. "Si, you know how I feel about those places. They creep me out."

"Just recently I was able to move him into a really nice place in Jersey. It's not creepy at all."

"It's just the idea of all those old, sick people...ugh."

She fought the urge to tell her sister to grow up. "This is Dad we're talking about. The man who raised you, remember?"

"According to what you told me the last time we talked, he's not even going to know I'm there. So what's the point?"

"We don't know that for sure. And he probably doesn't have much time left. This could be the last time you see him alive."

"Do you really think that's how I want to remember him?"

And did she think Sierra enjoyed bearing the brunt of his illness alone? Both emotionally and financially. "I'm sorry, but this is nonnegotiable. Either you promise, or it's the park bench for you."

Joy was quiet for several seconds, then she sighed again and said, "Fine, I'll go see him."

"And I'll ask Coop if you can stay." He had already done so much for her, had been so accommodating, she didn't want him to think that she was taking advantage of his hospitality. Yet she had little doubt that he would say yes. He seemed to like to keep up the "good guy" persona. On the bright side, Joy wouldn't be coming in for another week and a half, so Sierra could wait at least another week to ask him. Surely by then she would have worked off the last favor. She couldn't think of anything worse than being indebted to a man like Coop. There might just come a day when he called in the debt and demanded payment.

She would do this one thing for her sister's sake, but after that she would never ask Coop for a favor again.

"Dude, they're Russian models," Vlad said, but with his thick accent, *dude* came out sounding more like *dute*. "These babes are *super hot*. You can't say no."

As Coop had explained to his other former teammate, Niko, who had called him last night, he had turned over a new leaf. His days of staying out all night partying and bringing home women—even if they were *super hot*—were over. Vlad's call suggested that either he hadn't talked to Niko or he didn't think Coop had been serious.

"Sorry dude, you're going to have to count me out. Like I told Niko, I'm a family man now."

"But you find nanny, yes?"

"Yes, but I'm still responsible for the twins. They need me around."

Vlad grumbled a bit and gave him a serious ribbing for "losing his touch," but it didn't bother Coop. He said goodbye and reached down to pick up the toy Ivy had flung onto the sidewalk from the stroller and gave it back to her. The warm morning breeze rustled the newspapers on the table beside them on the café patio, and as he caught a glimpse of Sierra through the front window, standing in line, waiting to order them a cappuccino, Coop felt utterly content.

Besides, if the deal went through and he bought the team, the entire dynamic of his relationship with his former teammates would change. He would go from being their teammate and partner in crime to their boss. But he was ready to make that change.

He stuck his phone back in his shorts pocket and adjusted the stroller so that the twins were shaded from the morning sun. It would be another scorching day as July quickly approached, but at nine-thirty the temperature was an ideal seventy-five degrees. Most days, before the twins, he wouldn't have even been out of bed yet. In his twenties he could have easily spent the entire night out, slept a few hours, then arrived to practice on time and given a stellar performance. Recently though, the late nights out had been taking their toll. Parties and barhopping until 5:00 a.m. usually meant sleeping half the day away.

These days he was in bed before midnight—sometimes even earlier—and up with the sun. He had always been more of a night owl and had figured that the radical change to his schedule would be jarring, but he found that he actually liked getting up early. This morning he had woken before dawn, made coffee and sat on the rooftop terrace to watch the sun rise. He came back down with his empty cup a while later to find Sierra, still in her nightgown, fixing the twins their morning bottles.

She had jumped out of her skin when he said good morning, clearly surprised to find that he was already up. And though he'd tried to be a gentleman and not ogle her, he found himself staring at her cleavage again. And her legs. A woman as attractive as Sierra couldn't walk around half-naked with a man in the house and expect him to look the other way. And the fact that she hadn't tried to cover herself, nor did she set any speed records mixing the formula and filling the bottle, told him that maybe she liked him looking.

He glanced through the front window of the café and saw that she had inched ahead several feet in line and was only a few customers away from the counter. It had been his idea to stop for coffee and also his idea to come with her and the girls for their morning walk. He had just gotten back from jogging in the park as she was walking out the door. And it was an intrusion on her routine that had Sierra's panties in a serious twist. No big surprise considering the way she had been avoiding him the past week. He was sure it had everything to do with their conversation the day they moved her dad into the new nursing home. She could pretend all she liked, but she wasn't fooling him. She wanted him just as much as he wanted her.

A shadow passed over him and he looked up expecting Sierra, surprised to find an unfamiliar young woman in athletic attire standing by the table clutching a bottled water.

"Mr. Landon," she gushed, sounding a little out of breath. "Hi. I just wanted to say, I'm a *huge* fan."

Her long blond hair was pulled back in a ponytail and a sheen of sweat glazed her forehead. She must have been jogging past and noticed him sitting there. He wasn't really in the mood to deal with a fan, but he turned on the charm and said, "Thank you, Miss…"

"It's Amber. Amber Radcliff."

"It's nice to meet you, Amber."

Short and petite, she could have easily passed for seventeen, but he had the feeling she was closer to twenty-five. Just the right age. She was also very attractive, not to mention slender and toned. In fact, she was exactly the sort of woman he would normally be attracted to, yet when she smiled down at him, he didn't feel so much as a twinge of interest. She didn't even seem to notice that there was a stroller beside him with two infants inside.

"I've been a hockey fan, like, my *whole* life," she said, slipping uninvited into the empty seat across from him. "My dad has season tickets and we never missed a home game. I know you probably hear this all the time, but I am truly your number-one fan."

Her and a couple hundred thousand other fans. "Well, then I'm glad you stopped to say hi."

"The team just hasn't been the same since you retired. Last season was such a disappointment. I mean, they didn't even make the championships."

"I'm sure things will turn around next season." Because he would be in charge. Negotiations were currently at a standstill, but he was confident the current owner would come around and accept Coop's very reasonable offer.

Sierra appeared at the table, holding two cappuccinos and looking annoyed, not that he blamed her with some strange woman sitting in her chair. "Excuse me."

Amber looked up, gave Sierra a quick once-over, flashed her an oh-no-you-didn't look and said, "Excuse *me*, but I saw him first."

Seven

Sierra's brows rose, and Coop stifled a laugh. It was like that sometimes with fans. They figured just because they'd shelled out the cash to watch him bang a puck around the ice, they had some sort of claim on his personal time.

"Sierra," he said, "this is Amber. She's my biggest fan."

Sierra set the drinks down on the table with a clunk. "Charmed to meet you, Amber, but you're in my seat."

"Oh…sorry." Amber flushed a vivid shade of pink and awkwardly stood. "I didn't realize…"

"It's all good," Coop said, smiling up at her.

"Give my best to your dad, and tell him I said thanks for being such a loyal fan. And don't give up on the team. They'll come back strong next season, I guarantee it."

She mumbled a goodbye, tripping on the wheel of the stroller in her haste to get away.

"Well, that was interesting," Sierra said, sliding into her seat.

"It's the price you pay as a celebrity, I guess."

"Are all your fans that rude?"

"Some are a bit more aggressive than others, but no harm done. Besides, without the fans, I wouldn't have had a job. There wouldn't be a league, and I would have no team to buy." He took a sip of his cappuccino. "Delicious. Thanks."

"Were the twins okay?"

"Fine. Although Ivy keeps tossing her toy on the ground."

"Because she knows you'll pick it back up again."

"They do have me wrapped," he admitted, smiling down at them. And he would no doubt continue to spoil them until they were all grown up.

Sierra was quiet for a minute, a furrow in her brow as she gazed absently at her cup, running her thumb around the edge. She had seemed distracted all morning, as if there was something on her mind. Something bothering her. He would like to know if it was something he had done.

"Penny for your thoughts," he said.

She looked up. "You don't want to know."

Whatever it was, it looked as if it wasn't pleasant. If she was about to tell him she was quitting, after so adamantly vowing her dedication to the girls, he was going to be seriously pissed off. "Is there a problem?"

"Not exactly, no."

"Then what is it exactly?"

"I need a favor. A really big one. And I want you to know that you are under absolutely no obligation to say yes. But I promised I would at least ask."

"So ask me."

Ivy started to fuss, so Sierra reached into the

diaper bag for a bottle of juice and handed it to her, and when Fern saw it and began to fuss, she gave her one, too. "The thing is, my sister has an audition in New York so she's coming to visit."

"Do you need time off?"

She shook her head. "No. Anything we do together we can take the girls with us. The thing is, she would normally crash at my place. Unfortunately, I hadn't actually gotten around to telling her about my new job, so she just assumed she could stay with me. I guess she had to borrow money from her agent for the plane ticket, which is nonrefundable of course, and she doesn't have money for a hotel."

"So you want to know if she can stay with us."

"I wouldn't even ask, but Joy is a master at making me feel guilty. She threatened to sleep on a park bench."

"When? And how long?"

"She's flying in around noon tomorrow and staying a week. Which I know is a really long time."

He shrugged and said, "That's fine."

"You're sure you don't mind? Because you shouldn't be expected to invite complete strangers into your home."

"But she's not a stranger. She's your sister. And for the record, it's not a very big favor. If you asked me for a kidney, or a lung, that would be a big deal."

"But she's a stranger to you, and I feel like a dork for putting you on the spot."

He drew in a breath and sighed. Would she ever learn that he wasn't the ogre she seemed to have pegged him for? "Because we both know that deep down I'm a big fat jerk who would never do something nice for someone if not forced."

She shot him a look. "You know that isn't what I mean."

Sometimes she made him feel that way, as if she always expected the worst from him, despite the fact that in the two weeks he had known her, he had been nothing but courteous and accommodating and he hadn't once complained about anything. Someone must have done a serious number on her to make her so wary of trusting him. And trusting her own instincts.

"She's welcome to stay. And I'm not saying that because I feel obligated or because I'm trying to get into your pants."

Sierra bit her lip and lowered her eyes. "I didn't think that."

Not that he didn't want to. Get into her pants, that is. But not at the expense of losing her as the twins' nanny, and certainly not if she felt she owed him out of some sense of duty or repayment.

Ivy tossed her bottle this time, so far that it hit the chair leg of the elderly woman sitting at the next table. She leaned down to pick it up, carefully wiped it off with her napkin, then gave it back to Ivy, who squealed happily.

"What beautiful little girls," the woman said with a smile. "They look just like their mommy, but they have their daddy's eyes."

There didn't seem any point in trying to explain the situation, so Coop just smiled and thanked the woman. When he turned back to

Sierra, she looked troubled. Did the idea that someone might mistake the twins for their children disturb her so much? There were an awful lot of women out there who would be happy to earn that distinction. Clearly she was not one of them.

She leaned in and whispered, "You don't think they look like me, do you?"

"I can see why someone might think you're their mother."

"What do you mean?"

"You have similar skin tone and dark hair. But do you actually look alike?" He shrugged. "I don't really see it. And other than the fact that they have two eyes, the similarities between them and me pretty much stop there." He paused then said, "However, to see you with the twins, one would naturally assume they are yours."

She cocked her head slightly. "Why is that?"

"Because you treat them like a mother would treat her own children."

"I'm not sure what you mean. How else am I supposed to treat them?"

"Susan once told me that before she and Ash adopted the girls, she would sit at the park on her lunch break and watch the kids on the playground, hoping that some day she could watch her own kids playing there. She said she could always tell which of the adults were parents and which were nannies or au pairs. The parents interacted with their kids. She said you could just tell that they wanted to be there, that they cared. The caregivers, however, stood around in packs basically ignoring the kids and talking amongst themselves, occasionally shouting out a reprimand. She said that she made her mind up then that if she ever was blessed with a baby, she would quit working and stay home. And she did."

"It sounds like she was a really good mom," Sierra said softly.

"She was. So I'm sure you can imagine how I must have felt, knowing I had to hire a nanny, when Susan was so against the idea. Knowing that there was no way I could manage it alone, be both a mom and a dad to them. Feeling as if I was letting them down, as if I had failed them somehow. But then you came along, and in two weeks time you have surpassed my expectations by leaps and bounds. I can rest easy knowing that even when I can't be around, the twins are loved and well cared for. And even though they don't have a mom, they have someone who gives them all the love and affection a real mom would."

Sierra bit her lip, and her eyes welled up. He hadn't meant to make her cry. He just wanted her to know what an important part of their lives she had become and how much he appreciated it. And that it had nothing to do with wanting to get into her pants.

He reached across the table and wrapped his hand around hers, half expecting her to pull away. "So when I do something nice for you, it's because I want you to know how much we appreciate having you around. And I want you to be as happy with us as we are with you. I want you to feel like you're a part of our family. Unconventional as it is."

She swiped at her eyes with her free hand. "Thank you."

Ivy shrieked and threw her bottle again, and this time Fern followed suit. Coop let go of Sierra's hand to pick them up. "I think the natives are getting restless."

She sniffled and swiped at her eyes again. "Yeah, we should probably get moving."

Leaving their barely touched cappuccinos behind, they gathered their things and left the café. Coop had the overwhelming desire to link his fingers through hers, but with both her hands clutching the stroller handle he couldn't have anyway.

It defied logic, this irrational need to be close to her. To do things like skip meetings and ignore his friends just to spend time with her and the twins. He could have practically any other woman that he wanted. Women who showered him with flattery and clawed over each other for his attention. Women willing to be whatever and whoever he wanted just to make him happy.

Didn't it just figure that he had to fall for the one woman who didn't want him?

* * *

While the girls napped Sierra did laundry, wishing that this morning at the coffee shop had never happened.

Did Coop have to be so darned nice all the time? That stuff about her taking care of the girls was hands down the sweetest and kindest thing anyone had ever said to her. He was making it really hard for her to not like him. In fact, when he'd taken her hand in his…oh, my God. His hand was big and strong and had a roughness that should have been unpleasant, yet all she could think about was him rubbing it all over her. If they hadn't been in a public place, she might have done something completely insane like fling the table aside, plant herself in his lap and kiss him senseless. And then she would have divested him of the tank top and running shorts and put *her* hands all over *him*. The fact that he was still sweaty, unshaven and disheveled from his run should have been a turnoff, yet when she imagined touching his slick skin, feeling the rasp of his beard against her cheek, tasting the salty tang of his lips, she'd gone into hormone overload. She didn't even like sweaty, disheveled, unshaven men.

Why was she even thinking about this?

As good as it would be—and she *knew* it would be good—it would be a mistake. She still wasn't sure why he was attracted to her in the first place. Was it convenience—because he said himself that was how he normally chose his women? And what could be more convenient than a woman living right under his roof? Or was it the thrill of the chase fueling his interest? And if she let him catch her, just how long would it take before he got bored?

Probably not very long. And after he dumped her, she would find herself heartbroken, out of a job, homeless, and, worst of all, ripped away from her children. She simply had too much to lose. She had to do what was best for them.

The spin cycle ended and she tossed the damp linens into the dryer along with a dryer sheet and set it on High, then she dumped hers and the girls' dirty clothes in the washing machine.

She poured a scoop of detergent over the

clothes, then realized she was still wearing the shirt that Fern had flung a glob of pureed carrots all over at lunch. Ms. Densmore was at the market and Coop had left an hour ago for a meeting that he said would drag on until at least dinnertime, so figuring she could make it from the laundry room to her bedroom undetected in her bra, she pulled the shirt over her head, spritzed the spot with stain remover and tossed it in, too.

She shut the lid, started the machine and headed out of the laundry room...stopping dead in her tracks when she realized that Coop was in the kitchen.

For a second she thought that her mind must be playing tricks on her. No one's luck could be *that* bad.

She blinked. Then she blinked again.

Nope, that was definitely Coop, his hip wedged against the island countertop, his eyes lowered as he sorted through the mail he must have picked up on his way in. And any second now he was going to look up and see her standing there in her bra.

She could make a run for her bedroom, but she couldn't imagine doing anything so undignified, nor would she run back to the laundry room. Besides, Coop must have sensed her there because he looked up. And *he* blinked. Then he blinked again. Then his eyes settled on her breasts and he said, "You're not wearing a shirt."

She could have at least covered herself with her hands or grabbed the dish towel hanging on the oven door, but for some weird reason she just stood there, as if, deep down she *wanted* him to see her half-naked. Which she was pretty sure she didn't.

"Ms. Densmore is at the market, and I didn't think you would be home so soon," she said.

"My lawyer had to cut the meeting short," he explained, his gaze still fixed below her neck. "For which I plan to thank him *profusely* the next time I see him."

The heat in his eyes was so intense she actually thought her bra might ignite. "That explains it then."

"Out of curiosity, do you always walk around in your bra when no one is home?"

"My shirt had carrots on it from the girls' lunch. I threw it in the washing machine." When he didn't respond she said, "You could be a gentleman and look the other way."

He tossed the mail on the counter, but it hit the edge, slid off and landed on the floor instead. "I could. And I would if I thought for a second that you didn't like me looking at you."

There he went, reading her mind again. She really wished he would stop doing that. "Who says I like it?"

"If you didn't you would have made some attempt to cover yourself or leave the room. And your heart wouldn't be racing."

Right again.

"Not to mention you're giving off enough pheromones right now to take down an entire professional hockey team. And you know what that means."

She didn't have a clue, but the idea of what it might be made her knees weak. "What does it mean?"

"It means that I *have* to kiss you."

Eight

"Coop, that would be a really bad idea," Sierra said, but her voice was trembling.

Maybe it was, but right now, Coop didn't care. He crossed the room toward her and she held her breath. "All you have to do is tell me no."

"I just did."

He stopped a few inches from her and he could actually feel the heat radiating from her bare skin. "You said it would be a bad idea, but you didn't actually say don't do it."

"But that was what I meant."

"So say it."

She opened her mouth and closed it again.

Oh, yeah, she wanted him. He reached up and ran the pad of his thumb up her arm, from elbow to shoulder, then back down again. Sierra shivered.

"Tell me to stop," he said, and when she didn't say a word, when she just gazed up at him with lust-filled eyes, her cheeks flush with excitement, he knew she was as good as his.

He cupped her cheek in his palm, stroked with his thumb, and he could feel her melting, giving in. "Last chance," he said.

She blew out an exasperated breath. "Oh, for heaven's sake just shut up and *kiss* me already!"

He was smiling as he lowered his head, slanting his mouth over hers. When their lips touched, and her tongue slid against his, desire slammed him from every direction at once.

Holy hell.

Never in his life had he felt such an intense connection to a woman just from kissing her. Of course, he'd never met a woman quite like her. And he knew without a doubt that a kiss was never going to be enough. He wanted more...

needed it in a way he had never needed anything before.

She slid her arms around his neck, trying to get closer, but his arm was in the way. She broke the kiss and looked down at his crotch, which he was cupping in his free hand, then she looked up at him questioningly.

"Just in case I was wrong and you followed through on your threat."

"Threat?"

"You said that if I tried to kiss you I would be wearing the family jewels for earrings."

She laughed and shook her head. "You do realize, the fact that you thought I might actually do it makes you about a million times more appealing."

He grinned. "I told you, I'm irresistible."

"Coop, this is so wrong," she said.

He slid his hands across her bare back. Sierra sighed and her eyes drifted closed. "Nothing that feels this good could be wrong."

She must have agreed because she wrapped her arms around his neck, pulled his head down and kissed him. He might have taken her right there in the kitchen—he sure wanted to—but Sierra deserved better than sex on the counter or up against the refrigerator. She wasn't some woman he'd picked up in a bar or at a party. She was special. She wasn't in it for the cheap thrill of being with a celebrity. This would mean something to her, something profound. She deserved tenderness and romance, and when he did make love to her—which he would do, there was no longer any doubt about that—he wanted to take his time. He didn't want to have to worry about things like the twins waking up from their nap, which they were likely to do pretty soon. And though he could be content to stand there kissing and touching her until they did, Ms. Densmore could walk in at any moment. Not that he gave a crap what *she* thought, but he didn't want Sierra to feel embarrassed or uncomfortable. He really *cared* about her, which was just too damned weird.

Could he possibly be falling in love with her?

He didn't *do* love. Hell, he usually didn't do next week. To him women were nothing more than a way to pass the time. And not because of some psychological wound or fear of commitment. He hadn't been profoundly wounded by his parents' death or dumped by his one true love. He hadn't been double-crossed or cheated on. He had just been too focused on his career to make the time for a long-term relationship. He also hadn't met anyone he'd cared so deeply for that he couldn't live without them. But it was bound to happen eventually, wasn't it? What was the saying? There was someone for everyone? Maybe Sierra was his someone.

It took every bit of restraint he possessed to break the kiss, when there was really no guarantee she would ever let him kiss her again. He was giving her time to rethink this, to change her mind. But that was just a chance he had to take.

He took her hands, pulled them from around his neck and cradled them against his chest. "We should stop before we get too carried away."

She looked surprised and disappointed and maybe a little relieved, too. "The girls will be up soon."

"Exactly. And unless you want Ms. Densmore to see you half-naked, you might want to put a shirt on."

She looked down, as though she had completely forgotten she wasn't wearing one. "It might almost be worth it to see the look on her face."

From behind the kitchen they heard the service-entrance door open. If she wanted to see the look on Ms. Densmore's face, this was her chance. Instead she turned tail and darted from the room, ponytail swishing.

He chuckled at her retreating back. Not so tough, was she?

Ms. Densmore appeared with two canvas shopping bags full of groceries. He'd told her a million times that she could just order the groceries and have them delivered, but she insisted on walking to the market and carrying the bags back herself nearly every day.

When she saw him standing there she said, "I didn't expect you home so soon."

She looked tired, so he took the bags from her

and set them up on the countertop. "Meeting ended early."

While she put her purse away he poked through the bags, finding a variety of fresh vegetables, several jars of baby food and a package of boneless, skinless chicken breasts. "Chicken for dinner tonight?"

"Chicken parmesan," she said, looking curiously at the mail on the floor and stooping to pick it up. "We need to talk."

He could see by her expression, which was more troubled than sour, that there was a problem. "What's up?"

She put the chicken in the fridge, closed the door and turned to him. "I'm afraid I can't work for you any longer."

He knew she wasn't thrilled with having the twins around, but he didn't think she was miserable enough to quit. She may not have been a very nice person, but she was a good housekeeper and he hated to lose her. "Is there a specific problem? And if so, is there anything I can do to fix it?"

"I took this job because it fit certain criteria.

First, there were no children and not likely to ever be any, and second, you were rarely here. I like to be alone and left to my own devices. Since you brought the twins here everything has changed. I have to cook all the time and I hate cooking." She paused and said bitterly, "Not to mention that your nanny has been *tormenting* me."

He couldn't help laughing, which only made her glare at him. "I'm sorry, but *Sierra?* She's not exactly the tormenting type."

"She plays tricks on me."

"What kind of tricks?"

"She moves things around just to irritate me. She takes the milk off the door and puts it on the shelf and she rearranges things in the laundry room. She's petty and childish."

"I'll have a talk with her."

"It's too late for that. Besides, as long as the twins are around I won't ever be happy working here again."

He was sorry she felt that way, but neither did he want an unhappy employee. Or one who couldn't appreciate two sweet and beautiful infants. "So is this your two-week notice?"

"I got a new job and they need me to start immediately, so today is my last day."

"Today?" He couldn't believe she would leave him in a lurch that way.

"Let's not pretend that you wouldn't have eventually fired me. *She* would have insisted."

"Sierra? That's not her call."

"When she becomes the lady of the house it will be, and you know that will be the eventual outcome."

Coop had no idea that his feelings for Sierra were so obvious. And she was right. If he and Sierra did ever get married, she would insist that he get rid of Ms. Densmore, and of course he would because he would do practically anything she asked to make her happy.

"Don't worry," Ms. Densmore said. "You'll call a service and have a replacement before the week is out."

She was right. He just hated the idea of training someone new. "Do you mind my asking who you're going to be working for?"

"A diplomat and his wife. Their children are grown and they spend three weeks out of every month traveling. I'll pretty much be left alone to do my job."

"That sounds perfect for you."

"With the exception of the past month, it really has been a pleasure working for you, Mr. Landon. I just can't be happy here any longer. I'm too old and set in my ways to change."

"I understand."

"I'm sure Sierra can handle things until you find someone new."

He'd seen Sierra's bedroom. Housekeeping was a concept that seemed to escape her completely. Besides, with two infants to care for, she wouldn't have time to cook and clean, too. He needed someone within the next few days at the latest.

"Dinner will be ready at six-thirty," she said. "And I'm making a double recipe so there will be some left over. You can warm it for dinner later this week."

"Thanks."

She turned and busied herself starting dinner as Coop went to look for Sierra, to tell her what he was sure she would consider very good news. The nursery door was closed, meaning the girls were still asleep, so he knocked on Sierra's bedroom door instead. She opened it after a few seconds, and he was sorry to see that she had changed into a clean shirt.

"Have you got a minute?" he asked.

"Of course." She stepped aside and let him in. The bed was unmade, there was a bath towel draped over the chair, the desk was piled with papers and junk, and there was a pile of books and magazines on the floor next to the bed.

"Excuse the mess," she said. "I just can't ever seem to find the time to straighten up. After being with the girls all day I'm usually too exhausted to do much of anything."

Which meant doubling as housekeeper would be out of the question. "It's your room. If you want to keep it messy, that's your choice."

"I know it drives Ms. Densmore crazy, but she won't set foot in my room."

"Funny you should mention her. She's the reason I came to talk to you."

A worry line bisected Sierra's brow. "She didn't see me without my shirt on, did she?"

"Nope. But the way I hear it, you've been tormenting my housekeeper."

Uh-oh. Someone had tattled on her.

Sierra put on her best innocent look and asked, "What do you mean?"

Coop folded his arms, and though he was trying to look tough, there was humor in his eyes. "Don't even try to pretend that you don't know what I'm talking about. You know I can always tell when you're lying."

It was that mind-reading thing that he did. *So* annoying. "To call it 'torment' is an exaggeration. They were just...*pranks.* And you can't tell me that she didn't deserve it. She's so *mean.*"

"She just quit."

She gasped and slapped a hand over her heart. "She didn't!"

"She did, just now in the kitchen. This is her last day."

"Oh my gosh, Coop. I'm so sorry. I wanted to

annoy her, not make her leave. This is all my fault. Do you want me to talk to her? Promise to behave from now on?"

He grinned and shook his head. "You may have accelerated the process, but she would have left eventually anyway. She said she's been unhappy since the girls moved in. It wasn't what she signed on for. I hired her five years ago, when I was still playing hockey and barely ever here. She liked it that way."

"I still feel bad."

"Don't," he said, and gestured to a framed photo on the dresser. "Is that your mom?"

She smiled and nodded. It was Sierra's favorite shot of her. It was taken in the park, on a sunny spring afternoon. Her mom was sitting cross-legged in the grass on the old patchwork quilt they always used for picnics or at the beach, and she was looking up at the camera, smiling. "Wasn't she beautiful?"

He walked over and picked it up. "Very beautiful."

"She was always smiling, always happy. And it was infectious. You could not be in the same room and not feel like smiling. And she loved hugs, loved to snuggle. She and I would curl up on the love seat together every Sunday and read books or do crossword puzzles all day long. She was so much fun, always thinking up new adventures, trying new things. And my dad loved her so much. He never remarried. He didn't even date very often. I don't think he ever got over losing her. They never fought, never bickered. They had the perfect marriage."

"She was Asian?" Coop asked.

She nodded. "Her grandmother was Chinese. I used to wish that I looked more like her."

"You do look like her."

"I actually favor my dad more. Joy looks more like she did."

"You really miss her."

She nodded. "Every day."

He walked over to where she stood, took her hand and tugged her to him. She didn't put up a fight when he pulled her close and looped his arms around her, and it felt so *good* to lay her head on his chest, to listen to the beat of his heart. He was so big and strong and he smelled so yummy. And kissing him…oh, my. It was a little slice of heaven. And now it was just going to be the two of them, alone in the house—with the girls, too, of course. The idea made her both excited and nervous. She knew that kissing Coop had been a bad idea and that letting it go any further would be a mistake of epic proportions. But couldn't she pretend, just for a little while, that they actually had a chance? That an affair with Coop wouldn't ruin everything?

No, because for whatever reason, and though it defied logic, he seemed to genuinely like her. If all he cared about was getting her between the sheets, that's where they would be right now. And if she believed for a second that his feelings for her were anything but a passing phase, she wouldn't hesitate to drag him there herself. Unfortunately, she and Coop were just too different. It would never work.

She untangled herself from his arms and backed away. "We need to talk."

"Why do I get the feeling that I'm not going to like this?"

"What happened earlier, it was really, *really* nice."

"But…?"

"You and I both know that it's not going to work."

"We don't know that."

"I don't want to have an affair."

"I don't, either. I know this will be hard for you to believe, but I want more this time. I'm ready."

If only that were true. "How can you know that? You've known me what? Two weeks?"

"I can't explain it. All I know is that I've never wanted anyone the way I want you. It just…feels right."

His expression was so earnest, she didn't doubt he believed every word he said, and oh how she wished she could throw caution to the wind and believe him, too. But there was too much at stake. "I want you, too, Coop. And I don't doubt that it will be really, really good for a while, but eventually something will go wrong. You'll be unhappy, and I'll be unhappy, then things will get awkward, and though you'll hate to have to do it, you'll fire me because it will be what's for the best."

"I wouldn't do that."

"Yes, you would. You wouldn't have any other choice. Because think about it—what are you going to do? Dump me, then bring other women home right in front of me?"

"You're assuming it won't work. But what if it does? We could be really good together."

"That isn't a chance I'm willing to take." And there was no way to make him understand why without telling him the truth. And if she was looking for a way to get fired, that was it.

"So, the job is more important than your feelings for me?" he asked.

"The girls need me more than you do. And, if I lose this job, my father goes back into that hellhole he was in. I won't do that to him."

She could tell by his frown that he knew she was right, he just didn't want to accept it.

"I could fire you now," he said. "Then you would be free to date me."

She raised her brows at him. "So what you're saying is, if I don't sleep with you, you'll fire me?"

His frown deepened, and he rubbed a hand across his jaw. "When you say it like that it sounds really sleazy."

"That's because it *is* sleazy. It's also sexual harassment." Not that she believed his threat was anything but an empty one. He just wasn't used to not getting his way, but he would have to *get* used to it.

In her jeans pocket, the cell phone started to ring and she pulled it out to check the display. When she saw the number of the nursing home her heart skipped like a stone on a very deep, cold lake. That always happened when someone called about her dad because her first thought was inevitably that he had passed away. But they had lots of other reasons for calling her. So why, this time, did she have an especially bad feeling?

"I have to take this," she told Coop. "It's the nursing home."

She answered the phone, pulse pounding, her heart in her throat.

"Miss Evans, this is Meg Douglas, administrator of Heartland Nursing Center."

"Hi, Meg, what can I do for you?" she asked, hoping she said something simple, like there was a form that needed to be signed or a treatment they needed authorization for.

"I'm so sorry to have to inform you that your father passed away."

Nine

Coop changed the twins' diapers, wrestled them into their pajamas, then sat in the rocking chair with them, one on each arm, but neither made it even halfway through their bottle before they were sound asleep. It had been a busy afternoon of going first to the nursing home so Sierra could see her dad one last time, then to the funeral home to make the final arrangements. By the time they finally got home it was well past the twins' bedtime.

Ms. Densmore had left dinner warming in the oven and, in a show of kindness that surprised both him and Sierra, a note on the refrigerator expressing her sympathy for Sierra's loss. She wasn't so sorry that she offered to stay on a few days longer, though. Not that he expected her to.

He got up and carried the twins' limp little bodies to their cribs, kissed them and tucked them in. For a minute he stood there, watching them sleep, feeling so...peaceful. At first he'd believed that once he hired someone to care for the twins, life would go back to the way it had been before he got the girls. Two months ago, if someone had told him he would enjoy being a parent and be content as a family man, he would have laughed in their face. He figured he would be happy playing the role of the fun and cool uncle, showering them with gifts and seeing that they were financially set while someone else dealt with the day-to-day issues. The feedings and the diapers and all the messy emotional stuff that would later come with hormonal teenaged girls. He realized now that they deserved better than that. They deserved a real, conventional family.

Shutting the nursery door softly behind him,

he took the half-finished bottles to the kitchen and stuck them in the fridge, just in case one or both of the girls woke up hungry in the middle of the night. His and Sierra's dinner dishes were still in the sink, so he rinsed them, stuck them in the dishwasher and set it to run, recalling the days when he and his brother hadn't even been able to afford a dishwasher, and doing them by hand had been Coop's responsibility. He'd had to do his own laundry and cook three days a week, too. Maybe he was spoiled now, but he had no desire to return to those days, even temporarily. And with caring for the twins, her sister's visit and planning her dad's memorial service, Sierra definitely wouldn't have time to clean and cook. He didn't even know if she *could* cook.

He made a mental note to call a service first thing tomorrow and set up interviews for a new housekeeper as soon as humanly possible.

Though he normally drank wine in the evenings, a cold beer had a nice ring to it tonight, so he grabbed two from the fridge. He switched out the kitchen light, hooked the baby monitor to his belt and walked to the rooftop terrace where he'd sent Sierra while he got the twins settled for bed. She'd balked, of course, and gave him the usual line about how he had done enough already and she needed to do her job, but with a little persuasion she'd caved. It was strange, but lately he'd begun thinking of her as not so much a nanny, but the two of them as partners in raising the girls. And he liked it that way.

The sun had nearly set, so he hit the switch and turned on the party lights that hung around the perimeter of the terrace.

Sierra looked up from the lounge chair where she sat, her knees tucked up under her chin. When they got home she had changed into shorts and a tank top, and her feet were bare. He half expected her to be crying, but her eyes were dry. The only time she had cried today was when she'd gone into her dad's room.

"Are the twins in bed?" she asked.

"Out cold before their heads hit the mattress," he said, holding up one of the two beers. "Can I interest you in a cold one?"

"That actually sounds really good, thanks."

He twisted the tops off and handed her one of the bottles, then stretched out in the chair beside hers.

She took a long, deep pull on her drink, sighed contentedly and said, "That hits the spot. Thank you for helping me with the twins today and for driving me all over the place. I'm not sure how I would have managed without you."

"It was my pleasure," he told her, as he had the dozen other times she had thanked him during the day. He took a drink of his beer and cradled the bottle in his lap between his thighs. "How are you doing?"

"You know, I'm okay. I'm not nearly as upset as I thought I would be. I mean, I'm sad and I'm going to miss him, but the man who was my dad has been gone for a while now. No one should have to live that way. For his sake I'm relieved that it's over, that he's at peace." She looked over at Coop. "Does that make me a terrible person?"

"Not at all."

"I'm worried about Joy, though."

"She didn't take the news well?"

"No, she took it a little too well. She hasn't actually seen our father in almost four years. That's why I thought it was so important she see him when she was here. Now she'll never get the chance. I'm worried that she's going to regret it for the rest of her life. I asked if she wanted them to hold off on cremating him, so she could at least see him, but she said no. She doesn't want to remember him like that."

"It's her decision."

"I know." She took another swallow of beer and set the bottle on the ground beside her.

"Is there anything I can do? Do you need anything for the memorial? I know money is tight for you and your sister."

"I'm not letting you pay for my dad's memorial, so don't even suggest it."

"So what will you do?"

She shrugged. "I haven't quite figured that out yet."

"Is there insurance? If you don't mind my asking."

"There's a small policy. But after the medical bills and the funeral costs, there won't be much left. It's going to be at least a couple of weeks before I get a check."

"How about I give you an advance on next week's salary? Or more if you need it."

She hesitated, chewing her lip.

"I don't mind," he said. "And I'm pretty sure I can trust you to stick around."

She hesitated, picking at the label on her beer bottle. He didn't get why she was so wary of accepting his help. Isn't that what friendship was about? And he definitely considered her a friend. He would like to consider her much more than that if she would let him.

"You're sure it's not an imposition?" she asked.

"If it was, I wouldn't have offered."

"In that case, I would really appreciate it."

"I'll have the money wired into your account first thing in the morning."

"Thank you."

She was quiet for several minutes, so he said, "Penny for your thoughts."

"I was just thinking about the twins and how

sad it is that they won't remember their parents. At least I got fourteen years with my mom. I have enough wonderful memories to keep her alive in my mind forever. Or maybe, if the girls had to lose their mother and father, it was better now than, say, five or ten years from now. That way they don't know what they've missed. There was no emotional connection. Or maybe I'm totally wrong." She shrugged. "Who knows really."

"Losing Ash and Susan doesn't mean they won't have two loving parents."

She looked confused. "What do you mean?"

"The twins shouldn't be raised by an uncle. It's not good enough for them, either. They deserve a real family."

Her face paled. "Are you saying you plan to give them up?"

"No, of course not. I love them. I'm ready to settle down and be a family man. So I've decided to adopt them."

Sierra bit down hard on her lip, blinking back the tears that were welling in her eyes. She had wanted to believe that Coop had changed, that he would be a good father, but until just now she hadn't been sure. It felt as if an enormous weight had been lifted off her shoulders, as if she could breathe for the first time since she heard the horrible news of the crash. She was confident that no matter what happened between her and Coop, the twins would be okay. He loved them and wanted to be their father.

She looked over at Coop and realized he was watching her, worry creasing his brow. "I hope those are happy tears you're fighting," he said. "That you aren't thinking what a terrible parent I'll be and how sorry you feel for the girls."

More like tears of relief. "Actually, I was thinking how lucky they are to have someone like you." She reached for his hand and he folded it around hers. "And how proud Ash and Susan would be and how grateful."

"Come here," he said, tugging on her arm, pulling her out of her chair and into his lap. She curled up against his chest and he wrapped his arms around her, holding her so tight it was a little hard to breathe. And though she couldn't see his face, when he spoke he sounded a little choked up. "Thank you, Sierra. You have no idea how much that means coming from you."

She tucked her face in the crook of his neck, breathed in the scent of his skin. Why did he have to be so wonderful?

"You know the girls are going to need a mother," he said, stroking her hair. "Someone who loves them as much as I do. We could be a family."

"You hardly know me."

"I know how happy I've been since you came into our lives. And how much the twins love you." His hand slipped down to caress her cheek. "I know how crazy you make me and how much I want you."

Did he really want her, or was it that she was convenient? She fit into his new "family plan." And did it really matter? They could be a family. That was what the girls needed, and isn't that was this was about? "And if it doesn't work?"

He tipped her chin up so he could see her face. "Isn't it worth it to at least try?"

Yes, she realized, it was. They were doing it for the girls.

She turned in Coop's lap so she was straddling his thighs, then she cupped his face in her palms and kissed him. And he was right about one thing. Anything that felt this good couldn't be wrong.

She circled her arms around his neck, sliding her fingers through the softness of his hair, and as she did she could feel the stress leaching from her bones, the empty place in her heart being filled again. After what had been a long, stressful and pretty lousy day, he'd made her feel happy. In fact, she couldn't recall a time in her life when she had been as happy and content as she was with Coop and the twins. That had to mean something, didn't it? She had been trying so hard not to fall for him, maybe it was time to relax and let it happen, let nature take its course. Besides, how could she say no to a man who kissed the way he did? In no time his soft lips, the warm slide of his tongue, had her feeling all restless and achy.

Although she couldn't help noticing that kissing was *all* they were doing. She was practically crawling out of her skin for more, and he seemed perfectly content to run his fingers through her hair and caress her cheeks, but not much else. And when she tried to move things forward, tried to touch him, he took her hands and curled them against his chest.

Now that he had her where he wanted her, had he suddenly developed cold feet? Had he decided that he didn't want her after all? He was aroused, that much was obvious, so why wasn't he moving things forward?

She stopped kissing him. "Okay, what's the deal?"

He looked confused. "Deal?"

"You do know how to do this, right? I mean, it's not your first time or anything?"

One brow arched. "Is that a rhetorical question?"

"You're not doing anything," she said.

"Sure I am. I'm kissing you." He grinned that slightly crooked smile. "And for the record I'm thoroughly enjoying it. Is there something wrong with taking things slow? I want you to be sure about this."

Could she really blame him for being cautious? She was sending some pretty major mixed signals. Coop, though, had been pretty clear about what he wanted from the get-go.

"I want this, Coop," she told him. "I'm ready."

"Ready for what, that's the question," he said. "Am I going to get to second base? Third base? Am I going to knock it out of the park?"

She couldn't resist smiling. Were they really using sports euphemisms? "You can't hit a home run if you don't step up to the plate."

He grinned. "In that case, maybe we should move this party to my bedroom."

Ten

Watching Coop undress—and taking off her own clothes in front of him—was one of the most erotic and terrifying experiences of Sierra's entire life. He had insisted on keeping the bedside lamp on, and she couldn't help but worry that he wouldn't like what he saw. But if he noticed the faint stretch marks on her hips and the side of her belly, or that her tummy wasn't quite as firm as it had been before the twins, he didn't let it show. She was sure that he'd been with women who were thinner and larger busted and all around prettier than she was, yet he looked at her as though she was the most beautiful woman in the world.

Coop seemed completely comfortable in his nudity. And why wouldn't he? He was simply *perfect*. From his rumpled hair to his long, slender feet, and every inch in between. She'd never been crazy about hairy men, so the sprinkling of dark-blond hair across his pecks and the thin trail bisecting his abs was ideal. And all those muscles…wow.

"I've never been with anyone so big," she said.

One brow arched up as he glanced down at his crotch. "I always thought I was sort of average."

She laughed. "I meant muscular."

He grinned. "Oh, *that*."

But he wasn't *average* anywhere. "I just want to touch you all over."

"I think we can arrange that." He pulled back the blankets, climbed into bed and laid down, then patted the mattress beside him. "Hop in."

Feeling nervous and excited all at once, she slid in beside him. And though she wanted this more than he would ever know, as he pulled her close and started kissing her, she found she couldn't relax. Not that it didn't feel good. But he'd been with a lot of women, and she was willing to bet that compared to most of them she was, at best, a novice. Her experiences with her high school boyfriend had been more awkward than satisfying, and the handful of encounters she'd had while she was in nursing school hadn't exactly been earth-shattering. Her last sexual experience sixteen months ago with the twins' father had at most been a drunken *wham, bam, thank you ma'am* that they both regretted the minute it was over.

She wanted sex to be fun and satisfying. She wanted to feel that spark, that…*connection.* The sensation of being intrinsically linked— if such a thing really existed. Yet every new experience left her feeling disappointed and empty, faking her orgasms just to be polite, wondering if it was something she was doing wrong. What if the same thing happened with Coop? What if she couldn't satisfy him, either? What if she didn't live up to his expectations?

She had herself in such a state that when he cupped a hand over her breast, instead of letting herself enjoy it, she tensed up. He stopped kissing her, pushed himself up on one elbow and gazed down at her. "Now who's just lying there?"

Her cheeks flushed with embarrassment. She was naked, in bed with a gorgeous, sexy man and she was completely blowing it. "I'm sorry."

"Maybe we should stop."

She shook her head. "No. I don't want to stop."

"You have done this before, right?" he teased. "I mean, it's not your first time or anything."

If he wasn't so adorable, she might have slugged him. Instead she found herself smiling. "Yes, I've done this before. But probably not even close to as many times as you have."

He stroked her cheek, a frown settling into the crease between his brows. "And that bothers you?"

"No, of course not. I'm just worried that I won't measure up. That I'm going to disappoint you."

"Sierra, you won't. Trust me."

"But I *could*."

"Or I could disappoint you. Have you considered that? Maybe I've been with so many women because I'm such a lousy lay no one would sleep with me twice."

She couldn't help it, she laughed. "That is the dumbest thing I've ever heard."

"And for the record, I haven't slept with *that* many women. And not because I haven't had the opportunity. I'm just very selective about who I hop into bed with."

His idea of *not that many* could be three hundred for all she knew. And maybe that should have bothered her, but it didn't. Because she knew it was different this time. He was different. This actually meant something to him.

"What can I do to make you more comfortable?" he asked. "To assure you that your disappointing me isn't even a remote possibility."

"Maybe you could give me some pointers, you know, tell me what you like."

"You could kiss me. I like that. And you mentioned something about touching me all over. That sounds pretty good, too." He took her hand and cradled it against his chest, brushed his lips against hers so sweetly. "We'll take it slow, okay?"

She nodded, feeling more relaxed already. He had a way of putting her at ease. And good to his word he was diligent about telling her exactly what he wanted and where he liked to be touched—which was pretty much everywhere and involved using her hands and her mouth. And after a while of his patient tutoring, she gained the confidence to experiment all on her own, which he seemed to like even more. And Coop was anything but a disappointment. The man knew his way around a woman's body. He made her feel sexy and beautiful.

By the time he reached into the night table drawer for a condom, she was so ready to take that next step, she could barely wait for him to cover himself. He pressed her thighs apart, and she held her breath, but then he just looked at her.

"You're so beautiful," he said.

"Coop, please," she pleaded.

"What, Sierra? What do you want?"

Him. She just wanted him.

But he already knew because he lowered himself over her, and the look of pure ecstasy as he eased himself inside of her almost did her in. He groaned and ran his fingers though her hair, his eyes rolling closed, and she finally felt it, that connection. And it was even more intense, more extraordinary than she ever imagined. This was it. This was what making love was supposed to feel like. And whatever happened between them, as long as she lived, she would never forget this moment.

Everything after that was a blur of skin against skin, mingling breath and soft moans and intense pleasure that kept building and building. She wasn't sure who came first, who set whom off, but it was the closest thing to heaven on earth that she had even known. Afterward they lay wrapped in each other's arms, legs intertwined, breathing hard. And all she wanted was to be closer. They could melt together, become one person, and she didn't think that would be close enough.

In that instant the reality of the situation hit her like a punch to the belly. She hadn't planned it, hadn't expected it, not in a million years, but now there was no denying it. She was in love with Coop.

Coop was a disgrace to the male gender.

In his entire life he had never come first. Not once. He prided himself on being completely in control at all times. Until last night.

Watching Sierra writhe beneath him, hearing her moans and whimpers, had pushed him so far past the point of no return, a nuclear explosion wouldn't have been able to stop him. She made him feel things he hadn't realized he was even capable of feeling. For the first time in his life, sex actually meant something. He had reached a level of intimacy that until last night he hadn't even known existed. It should have scared the hell out of him, but he had never felt more content in his entire life.

"She's grabbing her suitcase right now," Sierra said from the passenger's seat, dropping her phone back in her purse. "She said to meet her outside of Terminal C."

Joy's flight had been a few minutes late, so

they had been driving around in circles while Joy deplaned and collected her luggage.

"I'm glad I fed the twins their lunch early today," Sierra said, looking back at them, sitting contentedly in their car seats. "And thank you again for picking Joy up. She could have taken the bus."

"It's no problem." He reached over and took her hand, twining his fingers through hers. "Besides, I owe you for last night."

She blew out an exasperated breath and rolled her eyes. "I don't know why you're making such a big deal out of this. It couldn't have been more than a few seconds before me."

That was a few seconds too long as far as he was concerned. "I don't lose control like that."

"I didn't even *notice.* I wouldn't have even known if you hadn't said something."

"Well, it's not going to happen again." And it hadn't. Not the second or third time last night, or this morning in bed, or in the shower. Not that there hadn't been a couple of close calls.

She shook her head, as if he were hopeless.

"Men and their egos. Besides, I sort of like knowing that I make you lose control."

"That reminds me, we need to stop at the pharmacy on the way home. We blew through my entire supply of condoms."

"We don't have to use them if you don't want to."

He glanced over at her. "You take birth control pills?"

"IUD."

Sex without a condom…interesting idea.

From the time he reached puberty Ash had drilled into Coop the importance of always using protection. Years before Coop became sexually active, Ash had bought him a box of condoms and ordered him to keep one in his wallet at all times, just in case. A thing for which Coop was eternally grateful, ever since one fateful night his junior year of high school when Missy Noble's parents were out for the evening and she jumped him on the den couch right in the middle of some chick movie whose title escaped him now.

Being the stickler for safety that Coop was,

not to mention the very real likelihood of being trapped into a relationship with an *accidental* pregnancy, he'd actually never had sex without one. But the idea was an intriguing one.

"I've been told that it feels better for the man that way," she said.

"Who told you that?"

"The men who tried to get me to do it without one, so I'm not sure if it's actually true or not. But logistically you would think so."

He looked over at her and grinned. "I guess we'll have to put that theory to the test, won't we? Just so you know, I get tested regularly."

"As a nurse I have to," she said.

"How's tonight looking for you?" he asked.

"With my sister here?"

"What we do in the privacy of our bedroom is our business."

"*Our* bedroom?"

"She's going to be sleeping in your room, so it just makes sense that you sleep in mine. And continue to sleep there when she's gone."

"You don't think we should take things a little bit slower?"

"You didn't seem to want to go slow last night."

"Having sex and me moving into your bedroom are two very different things."

"We're living together, Sierra. Where you sleep at this point is just logistics." He gave her hand a squeeze. "We're together. I want you to sleep with me."

She hesitated for a second, then nodded and said, "Okay."

Coop steered the SUV up to the C terminal and spotted Joy immediately. She was a taller, slimmer version of her big sister, with the same dark hair, though Joy's was wavier and hung clear down to her waist. Gauging by her long gauzy skirt, tie-dye tank, leather sandals and beaded necklaces, she was the free-spirit type. A total contrast to Sierra, who couldn't be more practical and conservative.

"There she is!" Sierra said excitedly.

Coop pulled up beside her and before he could even come to a complete stop Sierra was out the door.

He turned to the twins and said, "I'll be right

back, you two," then hopped out to grab Joy's bag. By the time he made it around the vehicle the sisters were locked in a firm embrace, and when they finally parted they were both misty-eyed.

Sierra turned to him. "Coop, this is my sister, Joy. Joy, this is Coop, my…boss."

Joy offered him a finely boned hand to shake, but her grip was firm. "I can't thank you enough for giving me a place to stay while I'm here. And for picking me up."

"I hope you don't mind squeezing in between the girls," he said.

"It beats takin' the bus."

He opened the door for Joy, and when both women were inside he grabbed the suitcase, heaved it into the back, then got back in the driver's side. Sierra was introducing her sister to the twins.

"That's Fern on the right and Ivy on the left," she said.

Joy shook each one of their tiny hands, which the twins seemed to love. "Nice to meet you, girls. And it's a pleasure to meet the man who my sister can't seem to stop talking about. Are you two a couple yet or what?"

"Joy!" Sierra said, reaching back to whack her sister in the leg. Then she told Coop, "You'll have to excuse my sister. She has no filter."

Joy just laughed and said, "Love you, sis."

Coop had known Joy all of about two minutes, but he had the distinct feeling that he was going to like Sierra's sister, and he didn't doubt that her visit would be an interesting one.

"You're sleeping with him," Joy said when the twins were down for a nap and they were finally alone in Sierra's bedroom…or Joy's bedroom as the case happened to be now.

"Yeah," she admitted. "As of last night."

"I kinda figured. There was a vibe." Joy heaved her suitcase onto the bed and unzipped it. "I knew he had to be hot for you to let your sister crash here."

"You don't pack light," Sierra said as she emptied the contents of her case onto the duvet.

"The guy I've been staying with is getting his place fumigated while I'm gone, so it just made sense to bring it all. Have you got a few extra hangers?"

Sierra pointed to the closet door. "In there."

Joy crossed the room and pulled the door open. "Holy mother of God, this closet is *huge*."

"I know. It's twenty times the size of the dinky closet in my apartment."

"I didn't realize that hockey players made so much money," she called from inside the closet, emerging with a dozen or so hangers.

"He's also a successful businessman. And he does tons of charity work. He sponsors teams in low- income areas and donates his time to hold workshops for young players. For some- one who had no interest in having kids of his own, he sure does a lot for them." She took note of the hippie-style clothing in a host of bright colors piled on the bed and asked Joy, "Did you bring something to wear to the memorial?"

Joy made a face. "I don't do black."

Sierra sighed, watching her hang her clothes and lay them neatly on the bed to be put in the closet. "It doesn't have to be black. Just not so…bright. If I don't have anything that fits you, we can go shopping tomorrow after your audition."

"You know I don't have any money."

"But I do. Coop advanced me a month's pay so I could pay for the memorial service."

"That was nice of him." She paused then said with a grin, "I suppose it had nothing to do with the fact that you put out."

She glared at her sister. "Not that it's any of your business, but he offered it *before* I slept with him. And only because I refused to let him pay for the memorial himself. He's always trying to do things like that for me."

"Wow, that must be rough. I know I would hate having a rich, sexy man try to take care of me. How can you stand it?"

Sierra leaned close to give her sister a playful swat on the behind. "I almost forgot what a smart ass you are."

Joy smiled. "I've been told it's one of my most charming qualities."

It could be. But then there were the times when it was just plain annoying.

"You know I like to take care of myself,"

Sierra said, and now that she no longer had to pay for their father's care, she could build herself a nice nest egg.

But how would that work exactly? Now that she and Coop were a couple, would he keep paying her, or would he expect her to care for the girls for free?

It was just one of many things that they would have to discuss. Like how far he wanted to take this relationship. Would she be his perpetual live-in girlfriend, or was he open to the idea of marriage some day? Would he want more kids, or were the twins going to be it for him? And if being with the twins meant sacrificing a little, wasn't it worth it?

She still wasn't one-hundred percent sure that moving into his bedroom at this early stage in their relationship was a good idea. Yes, technically they were living together, but sleeping in the same room after being lovers for less than twenty-four hours seemed to be pushing the boundaries of respectability.

"You know you're going to have to tell him the truth," Joy said.

And there lay her other problem—telling Coop she was the twins' birth mother. But what would be even more difficult would be telling him about the birth father. "I'll tell him when the time is right."

"Honestly, I'm surprised he hasn't figured it out on his own. They look just like you."

"We were at a café yesterday morning and the woman at the next table assumed we were the twins' parents. She said they looked just like me, but have their daddy's eyes."

"What did Coop say?"

"He doesn't see it, I guess."

"If you want this thing with Coop to go any-where, you have to be honest with him."

"I'm in love with him."

Joy looped an arm around her shoulder. "Si, you can't start a relationship based on lies. Trust me. I know this from personal experi-ence."

She laid her head on her sister's shoulder. "How did I get myself into this mess?"

"He'll understand."

"Will he?"

"If he loves you he will."

The trouble was, she didn't know if he loved her or not. He hadn't said he did, but of course, neither had she. It was one thing to feel it, but to actually put it out there, to leave herself so vulnerable…it scared her half to death. Especially when she was pretty sure that for him, his affection for her was in part motivated by his desire to do right by the twins. Was it her that he cared about, or was it the idea of what their relationship symbolized? His mental image of the perfect family.

If she did tell him the truth—*when* she told him—would his feelings for her be strong enough to take such a direct blow? And what if she didn't tell him? Would it really be so bad? What if knowing the truth changed his perception of his relationship to the girls? What if it did more damage than good? There was no way that he could ever find out on his own.

Joy took her hand and grasped it firmly, and

as if she were reading Sierra's mind said, "Si, you have to tell him."

"I will." Probably. Maybe.

"When?"

"When the time is right." If it ever was.

Eleven

Sierra and Coop had just gotten the girls set-tled for the night and into bed, and he had slipped into his office to answer the phone, when Joy exploded through the front door of the apartment in a whirl of color and exuber-ance and announced at the top of her lungs, "I got it!"

She'd had her audition that morning and had been waiting all day for a callback, pacing the apartment like a restless panther, whining all through dinner that if she hadn't heard some-thing by now, she wasn't going to and that her career as an actress was over. When Sierra couldn't take it a minute longer, she'd given her money and sent her out to find a dress for the memorial. Apparently she'd found one.

"That was fast," she said, setting the girls' empty bottles in the kitchen sink. "Let's see it."

"See it?" Joy said, looking confused.

"The dress." She turned to her sister, realizing that Joy wasn't holding a bag.

"I didn't get a dress. I got the *role*."

Confused, she said, "I thought if they were interested, they would have you in for a second audition."

"Normally they would, but they were so impressed with my performance and thought I was so perfect for the role, they offered me the part!"

"Oh my gosh!" Her baby sister was going to play the leading role in a movie! "Joy, that is so awesome!"

She threw her arms around her sister and hugged her, and that's how Coop found them a second later when he came out of his office.

"I heard shouting," he said.

"Joy got the part," Sierra said.

"Hey, that's great!" Coop said, looking genuinely happy for her. "I hope you'll remember us little guys when you're a big Hollywood star."

Joy laughed. "Let's not get ahead of ourselves. Although this could open some major doors for me. And honestly, I'm just thrilled to have a job. I had to give up my waitressing job to come here. If it wasn't for my friend Jerry letting me stay at his place, I would be out on the streets until filming starts."

"When is that?" Sierra asked.

"Early August in Vancouver, and we wrap in September."

"I've played in Vancouver," Coop said. "You'll love it there."

"Oh, my God!" Joy said, practically vibrating with excitement. "I can't believe I actually got it!"

Joy was usually so negative and brooding, it was nice to see her happy for a change. Sierra was about to suggest they celebrate when the doorbell rang.

"That's Vlad and Niko," Coop said, heading

for the door. "Former teammates. They called to say they were stopping by."

He pulled the door open and on the other side stood two very large, sharply dressed Russian men. One looked to be around Coop's age and the other was younger. Early twenties maybe. Both men smelled as if they had bathed in cologne.

Sierra heard Joy suck in a quiet breath and say, "Yum."

"Ladies, this is Vlad," Coop said, gesturing to the older man, "And this is Niko. Guys, this is my girlfriend, Sierra, and her sister, Joy."

Neither man could mask his surprise. Sierra was assuming that men like Coop didn't usually have "girlfriends."

"Is good to meet you," Vlad said with a thick accent, addressing Sierra, but Niko's eyes were pinned on Joy, and she was looking back at him as if he were a juicy steak she would like to sink her teeth into. If she weren't a vegetarian, that is.

"You come out with us," Vlad told Coop.

"Big party at the Web's place. You bring girl-friend. And sister, too."

"The Web?" Sierra asked.

"Jimmy Webster," Coop told her. "The Scorpions goalie. He's known for his wild parties. And thanks for the invitation, guys, but I'm going to have to pass."

"You must come," Vlad said. "I don't take no for answer."

Coop shrugged. "I have to be here for the twins."

"But you have nanny for twins," Vlad said.

"Actually, I'm the nanny," Sierra said, which got her a curious look from both men. She could just imagine what they were thinking. How cliché it must have appeared. The starry-eyed nanny falls for the famous athlete.

Sierra turned to Coop. "You go. I'll stay here and watch the girls."

"See," Vlad said. "Is okay. You come with us."

Instead of darting off to change, Coop looped an arm around her shoulder and said, "No can do. Sorry."

Sierra wasn't exactly crazy about the idea

of him going to a party where there would be women more beautiful and desirable than her lobbying to be his next conquest, but it was something she would just have to get used to. She couldn't expect him to give up his friends and his social life just because she lacked the party mentality. "It's really okay. Go be with your friends."

"Web's parties are really only good for two things—getting wasted and picking up women. I'm well past my partying days, and the only woman I want is standing next to me."

If he was just saying that to keep from hurting her feelings, she couldn't tell. He looked as though he meant it, and it made her feel all warm and fuzzy inside.

"How about you?" Niko said, his gaze still pinned on Joy. "You come to party."

It was more of a demand than a question, which would have annoyed Sierra, but Joy smiled a catlike grin and said, "I'll go grab my purse."

"Do you think she'll be okay?" Sierra asked after they left, Joy draped on the younger player's arm. Not that she didn't think Joy could hold her own, but she didn't know the Russian guys, and she was still Sierra's baby sister. She would always feel responsible for her.

"Those guys are harmless," Coop assured her. "It looks as though she already has Niko wrapped around her finger."

"Men have always been helpless to resist her beauty." And usually got way more than they bargained for. Joy was beautiful and sexy, but she was also moody and temperamental. It would take a special kind of man to put up with her antics. In the long term, that is.

"Why don't you come sit down?" Coop said, nudging her toward the couch.

"Let me finish up in the kitchen real quick." She had been doing her best to keep things tidy until Coop found a new housekeeper, but she'd been tied up a good part of the day finalizing the details for the memorial, and already clutter was beginning to form on every flat surface and the furniture had developed a very fine layer of dust.

"Leave it for tomorrow," he said, trying to

steer her toward the couch, but she ducked under his arm. She already had a full day tomorrow.

"Five minutes," she said, heading into the kitchen.

Coop stretched out in his chair and turned on ESPN as she finished loading the dishwasher and wiped down the countertops. Ms. Densmore had kept them polished to a gleaming shine, but under Sierra's care they were looking dull and hazy. She poked through the cleaning closet for something to polish them, but after reading the label decided it was too much work to start tonight. She fished out one of those disposable duster thingies instead, but as she started to dust the living room furniture Coop looked up from the sports show he was watching and said, "What are you doing? Come sit down and relax."

"The apartment is filthy," she said.

"And we'll have a new housekeeper in a few days." He reached over and linked his hand around her wrist, pulling her down into his lap. He took the duster and flung it behind him onto the floor, creating an even bigger mess of the room. Then he pressed a soft kiss to her lips. "This should be our alone time."

And she still felt guilty for making him stay home or making him feel as though he had to. "Are you sure you're not upset about missing the party? Because you can still go."

"I didn't want to go. If it had been one of the married guys having a party, then sure, but only if we got a sitter and you came with me."

"I'm really not the party type."

"You wouldn't like a party where the couples are all married and instead of getting hammered and hooking up, they talk about preschools and which diapers are the most absorbent?"

"They do not."

"They do, seriously. I used to think they were totally insane. What could be more boring? Now I totally get it."

"I guess I wouldn't mind a party like that," she said.

"The married guys on the team are very family oriented, and I think you would like the wives. They're very down-to-earth and friendly. Everyone gets together for barbecues during the summer. We should go sometime."

That actually sounded like fun. There was only one problem. "You said it's the players and their wives, but I'm not your wife."

"Not yet. But there are girlfriends, too. The point is, it's not a meat market."

Sierra's breath backed up in her chest. Did he really just say "not yet," as in, someday she would be? Was he actually suggesting that he intended to make her an honest woman?

"We don't have to go," Coop said.

"No, I'd like to."

"Are you sure? Because you just had a really funny look on your face."

"It wasn't that. I just didn't know… I didn't realize how you felt about that. About us."

His brow wrinkled. "I'm not sure what you mean."

"I said 'I'm not your wife,' and you said 'not yet.'"

His frown deepened. "Are you saying that you wouldn't want to be my wife?"

"No! Of course not. I just didn't know that you would *want* me to be. That you ever wanted to get married. You strike me as the perpetual bachelor type."

"It's not as if at some point I decided that I would never get married. To be honest, I was jealous as hell of Ash. He found the perfect partner for himself, and they were so happy. I just haven't had any luck finding the right one for me. I may not be ready for a trip down the aisle right now, but eventually, sure. Isn't that what everyone wants?"

The question was: Did he want to take that trip with her? That was definitely what he was implying, right? And how long was eventually? Months? A year? Ten years? She'd never been in a relationship serious enough to even consider marriage, so how long did it take to get to the wedding? Or the proposal? After he got down on one knee, how long before they said *I do?*

"You know," he said, nuzzling her cheek, nibbling her ear, sending a delicious little shiver of pleasure up her spine. "You came to bed so late last night we never got to test out that condom theory."

She and Joy had sat up until almost three last night talking, and Coop had been sound asleep by the time she slipped into bed beside him. "But we have the place all to ourselves now," she said, turning in his lap so she was straddling him. She reached down and tugged at the hem of his T-shirt, pulling it up over his head. He was so beautiful, it was still a little hard to believe that a man like him would want someone like her. But she could feel by the hard ridge between her thighs that he did.

She pulled her shirt up over her head and tossed it on the floor with his. He made a rumbly sound in his throat and wrapped his big, warm hands over her hips.

"You are the sexiest woman on the planet," he said, sliding his hands upward, skimming her bra cups with his thumbs. He sure made her feel as if she were. So why did she have the nagging feeling that it wasn't destined to last, that she was a novelty, and at some point the shine would wear thin? That he was going to miss the parties and the running around.

Either way, it was too late now. She was hooked. She loved him, and maybe someday he would learn to love her, too. They could make this work. She would be such a good wife, and keep him so happy, he wouldn't ever want to let her go.

For the twins' sake she had to at least try.

Holy freaking hell.

Coop lay spread-eagled on his back in bed, the covers tangled around his ankles, sweat beading his brow, still quaking with after-shocks from what was hands down the most intense orgasm he'd ever had. Making love to Sierra without the barrier of latex, to really feel her for the first time, was the hottest, most erotic experience of his life.

"So is it true?" Sierra asked, grinning down at him, still straddling his lap, her skin rosy with the afterglow of her own pleasure. Looking smug as hell. "Is it better without a condom?"

He tried to scowl at her, but he felt so good, so

relaxed, he couldn't muster the energy. "You're evil," he said instead, and her smile widened. He should have known, when she insisted on being on top, that she was up to something. That she intended to humiliate him again. But even he couldn't deny it was the most pleasurable humiliation he'd ever had to endure.

"You beat me by what, five seconds?" she said.

No thanks to her. He had obviously been having trouble holding it together, but instead of giving him a few seconds to get a grip, she had to go and do that thing with his nipples, which of course had instantly set him off.

For someone who claimed not to have much experience with men, she sure knew which buttons to push.

"It's the principle of the thing," he told her. "The man should never come first."

"That's just dumb."

"Yeah, well, as soon as I can breathe again, you're in trouble." He wrapped his arms around her and pulled her down against his chest, kissing the smirk off her face. Sierra slid down beside him, curling up against his side. It felt as if that was exactly where she belonged. Beside him. It was astounding to him what adding an emotional connection could do to crank up the level of intimacy. He had never felt as close to anyone, as connected to another person. He had no doubt that she would be the perfect wife. A good mother, a good friend and an exceptional lover. And he knew that once she met his friends, and trusted them enough to drop her guard a little, she would fit right in.

Yeah, she wasn't much of a housekeeper, and her expertise in the kitchen was pretty much limited to things she could heat in the microwave, but he could hire people to do that. In all the ways that counted, she was exactly the sort of woman he would want as a companion. She was predictable and uncomplicated…what you see is what you get. And she was as devoted to the twins, to taking care of them, as he was. Never had he imagined finding someone so completely perfect. He'd never been one to believe in cosmic forces, but he was honestly beginning to think that fate had brought them together. She had been thrust into some pretty rotten circumstances, and like him she had come out swinging. In fact, in a lot of ways they were very much alike.

So why couldn't he shake the feeling that she was holding something back? That she didn't completely trust him. He was sure it had more to do with her own insecurities than anything he had done. She just needed time. Time to trust him and believe him when he said that he wanted to make this work. That he wanted them to be a family.

But as her hand slid south down his stomach, he decided that he had plenty of time to worry about that later.

Twelve

When Sierra got back from her morning walk with the twins the next day, Joy was awake—a surprise considering she didn't wander in until after 4:00 a.m.—and she was dusting the living room dressed in yoga pants and a sport bra. And she somehow made it look glamorous.

"You don't have to do that," Sierra told her, taking the twins from the stroller and sitting them in their ExerSaucers.

"Someone has to do it."

"I'll get around to it."

Joy shot her a look. "No you won't. You hate cleaning."

She couldn't deny it. People would naturally think that Joy, being such a free spirit, would be the one with the aversion to cleaning, and Sierra, the responsible one, would be neat as a pin, but the opposite was true.

"If you decide to have anyone come back here after the memorial tomorrow, it should at least be tidy," Joy said.

"Well, thank you. I'm sure Coop will appreciate it."

"Consider it payment for letting me stay here. And introducing me to Niko. He's too adorable for words."

"How was the party?"

"Wild. Those hockey dudes really know how to have a good time."

Sierra walked into the kitchen to fix the twins' bottles and nearly gasped when she realized that it was spotless and the granite had been polished to a gleaming shine. "Oh my gosh! It looks amazing in here!"

Joy shrugged, like it was no big deal. "I like cleaning. It relieves stress."

She took after their dad in that respect. And

Sierra was like their mom, who was more interested in curling up with a book or taking a long, leisurely walk in the park or working in the local community garden. Their home had been messy but happy. Even when they found the cancer, it hadn't knocked her spirits down, or if it had, she never let it show. Not even when she had been too sick from the chemo to eat or when the pain must have been excruciating. She had taken it in stride up until the very end.

It would be twelve years in September, and though the pain of losing her had dulled, Sierra still missed her as keenly as she had that first year. She missed her warm hugs, and her gentle voice. Her playful nature. Why sit inside cleaning bedrooms and doing homework when there was a world full of adventures to explore? Sierra only hoped that she would be as good a mother, as good a wife as her mom had been.

She poured juice into bottles and carried them to the living room for the twins. "Do you still miss her?" she asked Joy.

"Miss who?" she asked, though Sierra had the feeling she knew exactly who she meant.

"Mom. It'll be twelve years this fall."

Joy shrugged. "I guess."

"You *guess?*" How could she *not* miss her?

"You were always closer with her than I was."

"What are you talking about? Of course I wasn't."

Joy stopped dusting and turned to her. "Si, come on. Half the time she didn't even know we were there, and the other half she spent doting on you. You two were just alike, she used to say."

"Yes, she and I were more alike, but she didn't love you any less."

"Didn't it ever bother you that the entire world seemed to revolve around her? Dad ran himself ragged working two jobs, and half the time she wouldn't even have dinner fixed when he got home. We would end up eating sandwiches or fast food."

"Not everyone is a good cook," Sierra said.

"But she didn't even try. And the apartment was always a mess. It was as if she was allergic to cleaning or something. Dad got one day a week off, and he would have to spend it vacuuming and picking up all the junk she and you left all over."

Sierra couldn't believe she would talk about their mom like that, that she even felt that way. "She was a good wife and mother. Dad adored her."

"She was a flake, and dad was miserable. My bed was right next to the wall and I could hear them fighting when they thought we were asleep."

"All couples fight sometimes."

"Sure, but with them it was a nightly thing."

Sierra shook her head. "No, they were happy."

"Look, believe me or don't believe me, I really don't care. I know what I heard. I don't doubt that Dad loved her, but he *wasn't* happy."

Maybe their mom could be a little self-centered at times, but she loved her family, all of them equally, despite what Joy believed. She did her best. If that wasn't good enough for Joy, that was *her* problem.

Joy's cell phone, which was sitting on the coffee table, started to ring and she dashed over to grab it.

"It's Jerry!" she said excitedly, who Sierra remembered was the "friend" she had been staying with. "Did you get my message? I got the part!" She flopped down on the couch and propped her feet on the coffee table. "I know! Isn't it awesome… No, not until August. Maybe you can come visit me there."

There was a pause, and Joy's smile began to disintegrate. "No, I don't have anyone else I can stay with until then. Why?" Joy sat up as outrage crept over her features. "What do you mean she's moving back in? You told me that you're getting divorced!"

Another married boyfriend? What was Joy's fixation with unavailable men? Why couldn't she find a nice, single guy? One who wouldn't screw her over and break her heart.

Joy jerked to her feet, shouting into the phone, "You sleazy-ass son of a bitch. You've been planning this since before I left, haven't you? You were never going to fumigate. You just wanted my stuff out so you could move her back in. I could have had a totally hot Russian guy last night, but I was being faithful to you, you big jerk! He was young and hot and I'll bet he doesn't have any of your *performance* problems."

Whoa. Maybe this was a conversation best kept private. Not that she thought Joy gave a damn if Sierra heard. She liked that element of drama. *Clearly.*

Joy listened, looking angrier by the second, then growled, "Take your apologies and shove them, you heartless bastard." She disconnected the call, blew out a frustrated breath and said, "Well, *crap.*"

"You okay?" Sierra asked.

Joy collapsed back onto the couch. "It's official, I'm homeless."

"I meant about Jerry. You were dating him?"

She shrugged. "I don't know if you would actually call it dating. He gave me a place to stay and I kept him company."

Sierra could just imagine what that entailed.

"I mean, I liked him, but it's not as if we

had some sort of future. He's kind of old to be thinking long term."

"How old?"

"Fifty-two."

Sierra's jaw dropped. "He's *thirty* years older than you?"

"Like I said, I didn't want to marry the guy. It was just…convenient."

Sierra raised a brow.

"For *both* of us. He liked having a much younger companion to flaunt, and I liked having a roof over my head."

"You liked him enough to be faithful to him," Sierra said.

Joy shrugged. "He was a nice guy. Or so I thought."

Sierra had the feeling Joy cared about him more than she wanted to admit. "So, what are you going to do?"

"I have no idea. I gave up my waitressing job for this trip and the film doesn't start shooting until the end of August. Even if I could find another job it would be a month before I could afford first and last months' rent."

"Can't you get some sort of signing bonus?"

She shook her head. "It's very low budget. My salary will barely cover living expenses."

"So what are you going to do? Stay with another friend?"

"When you mooch off everyone you know, eventually you run out of people to mooch off. But don't worry," she said, pushing herself back up off the couch and grabbing the duster. "I'll figure something out. I always do."

Sierra was a little surprised that Joy hadn't asked if she could stay with her and Coop. Maybe she knew Sierra would say no. It was one thing to have her stay for a short visit, but for more than a month? If she had her own place, no problem, but she would never ask Coop for that kind of favor.

Joy was a big girl. She was going to have to figure this one out on her own.

Coop sat at the conference table in his lawyer's office, fisting his hands in his lap, struggling to keep his cool, to keep his expression passive.

"We agreed on a price," he told his former boss, Mike Norris, the current owner of the New York Scorpions. A price that had been a couple million less than what he wanted today.

The arrogant bastard sat back in his chair, an unlit cigar clamped between his teeth, wearing a smug smile. Flanking him were his business manager and his lawyer, both of whom were as overweight, out of shape and devoid of human decency as Mike.

"My team, my terms," Mike said. "Take it or leave it."

He knew how badly Coop wanted it, and he was trying to use it to his advantage. The paperwork had been drawn up and Coop came here thinking that they would be signing to lock in the terms. But Mike had gotten greedy. Coop should have seen this coming, he should have known the son of a bitch would pull something at the last minute.

At the price they had agreed on last week, buying the team would have had its risks, but it was still what he considered a sound investment. At the price Mike was demanding now,

Coop would be putting too much on the line. His conservative nature with money was responsible for his healthy portfolio. If it were just his financial future hanging in the balance, he might say what the hell and go for it, but he had the twins to consider now. Sierra, too, although he doubted his money was a motivating factor in her feelings toward him. In fact, he was pretty sure she was intimidated by it. It was one of her most appealing qualities.

"Why the hesitation, Landon?" Mike said. "You know you want it, and we all know you can afford it. If you're hesitating because you think I'm going to back down, it ain't gonna happen." He leaned in toward the table, his belly flab preventing him from getting very close. "Just say yes and we've got a deal."

Even if he had planned to say yes, to give Mike what he wanted, that would have killed the deal.

He wanted that team, wanted it more than anything in his life, and giving it up would be one of the hardest things he would ever have to do, but it would be for the best. He glanced over at Ben, whose expression seemed to say that he knew what was coming, then Coop pushed back from the table and stood. "Sorry, gentleman, but I'm going to have to pass."

He started for the door and Mike called after him, sounding a little less smug now. "This deal is only good this afternoon. After today the price goes up again."

Mike thought Coop was bluffing. He wasn't. And though Coop wanted to tell him to shove his threat where the sun don't shine, he restrained himself. He was dying to see Mike's expression as he left, but he resisted the urge to turn and look as he walked out the conference room door and down the hall to Ben's office.

He sat down, taking long, deep breaths, fisting his hands in his lap when what he wanted to do was wrap them around that smug bastard's throat.

Ben walked in the office several minutes later, presumably after seeing the other men out.

"Coop, I'm sorry. I had no idea they were going to pull that."

Coop shrugged. "It's not your fault."

"You have every right to be furious. I know how much you wanted this."

It wasn't just about owning the team and the money that it would bring in. He cared about those guys. Mike was an old-school business-man who, until he bought the team five years ago, had never even been to a hockey game. For him it was nothing more than an investment. He knew nothing about the game and had been running the team into the ground since he took over. He didn't care about the players—his only goal was to pad his pockets. And the players knew it. They also knew that when Coop was at the helm, things would change. They would be back on top.

He felt as if he was letting them down.

"I don't know what I'm going to tell the guys."

"You're going to tell them exactly what hap-pened. Norris screwed you. But don't con-sider this over. Not yet. You should have seen Norris's face when you walked out. He really thought he had you. I wouldn't be too surprised if we get a call from him in a day or two backing down on his price."

"If he does, make it clear that I'm not paying him a penny over what we originally agreed on."

"There's something else we need to talk about," Ben said, and the furrow in his brow made Coop think that whatever it was, it wasn't good. "I didn't want to say anything before we signed the deal, and now probably isn't the best time after what happened in there…"

Whatever it was, it couldn't be much worse than what he'd just gone through. "Just tell me."

"A source at the National Transportation Safety Board has informed me that the official report on the plane crash is going to be released Monday."

Coop's heart clenched in his chest, then climbed up into his throat. "Did this source tell you what's in the report."

"They're calling it pilot error."

"No way!" Coop shot up from his seat. "No way it was pilot error. Your source must have it wrong."

"According to the report there were narcotics recovered from the scene."

"Which wouldn't surprise me in the least. Susan hurt her back a week before the trip. She ruptured a disc. It was so painful she couldn't even pick the twins up. I'm sure her doctor can confirm that. And she wasn't flying the plane."

"He said they found narcotics and marijuana in both Susan and Ash's systems."

No way. He knew that Ash and Susan smoked occasionally, but Ash would *never* take anything and then operate a plane. "I don't believe it. I know my brother, Ben. Ash would never take drugs and fly."

"We'll know more when we get a copy of the report, but if it's true, all hell is going to break loose and the vultures are going to descend. You might even want to get out of town for a few days, or even a week or two. Until things die down."

With the deal falling through he had nothing pressing to keep him in town, and frankly, he could use a vacation. "We have the memorial for Sierra's dad tomorrow, but after that there's nothing keeping me in the city. I think a trip to my place in Cabo might be in order."

"How is it working out with Sierra?"

Coop scrubbed a hand across his jaw. "Um… well, better than I anticipated, actually."

Ben narrowed his eyes. "Oh, yeah, how much better?"

A smile tugged at the corners of his mouth. "She moved into my bedroom two nights ago."

"I distinctly recall you telling me that you weren't going to sleep with her."

"It wasn't something I planned. But she's just so…extraordinary."

"So it's serious?"

"Yeah, I think so. She's everything I didn't realize that I wanted in a woman."

Ben grinned and shook his head. "I had no idea you were such a romantic, Coop. You should needlepoint that on a pillow."

"Who'd have thought, right? But she's smart and funny and beautiful, and the twins love her. And she doesn't seem to give a damn about my money."

"Should I start drafting the prenup?"

"Let's not get ahead of ourselves." Besides, he couldn't imagine making Sierra sign one of those. It would be the same as saying that he didn't trust her. He was a pretty good judge of character and as far as he could tell, she didn't have a deceitful bone in her body.

Ben eyed him warily. "You do plan to have a prenup, right? Assuming that you're going to marry her eventually."

"I'm definitely going to marry her. Eventually. But as far as a prenup...I don't think that's going to be necessary. She's not after my money."

"Not now, maybe..."

"I trust her, Ben."

"It's not about trust. It's about protecting you both in the case of a divorce."

"That would never happen. She's it for me. I know she is."

"One of my partners specializes in divorce, and the horror stories he could tell you—"

"That wouldn't happen to me and Sierra. We

both come from very stable, loving homes. We aren't products of divorce. Her parents were happily married and so were mine. Whatever problems we might have, we would work them out."

"You're rationalizing."

"I'm being realistic."

"So am I."

"To even ask would feel like a betrayal. It would be like saying that I don't trust her."

"If the two of you have such a great relationship, I would think she would understand. The least you could do is ask. If she balks, I might reconsider my position on the matter."

"She won't."

"Promise me that you'll at least consider it."

"I will. And like I said, we have no immediate plans to get hitched. I haven't even proposed yet."

"Just keep it in mind when you do."

In a way Coop wished he hadn't said anything to Ben about marrying her. What with the sour deal, the accident report and Ben's prenup lecture, Coop left his office feeling down-right depressed.

But on the bright side, things couldn't get much worse.

Thirteen

Coop caught a cab back home, getting out a block early so he could pick up a bouquet of flowers for Sierra from a street vendor. Remembering that they had never really had a chance to celebrate Joy's new job, he got her one, too. He walked the rest of the way home, the sun's heat beating down on his shoulders and back, melting the tension that had settled into his bones. Which made a week or two in a sunny locale sound even more appealing. If they left Sunday, they would be long gone before the backlash from the NTSB report hit the media.

The doorman greeted Coop as he headed inside and he had the elevator all to himself on the ride up. He opened the apartment door and the scent of something delicious tantalized his senses. Something that smelled too good to have come from a microwave. He dropped his keys on the entryway table and walked into the living room, realizing that not only was someone cooking, but also someone had cleaned. The apartment was spotless.

Sierra appeared from the hallway, jerking with surprise when she saw him standing there. "Hey! Hi, I didn't hear you come in."

At the sight of her, his heart instantly lifted, a smile tugged at his lips and all the crap that happened today, all the rotten news, didn't seem so terrible any longer. "I just got here."

"I just put the girls down for a nap." Her eyes settled on the bouquets he was carrying. "Nice flowers."

"One for you," he said, handing her the larger of the two.

"Thank you!" She pushed up on her toes and

kissed him. "I can't even remember the last time someone gave me flowers."

"This one is for Joy," he said of the second bouquet. "To say congratulations. Is she here?"

"She ran down to the market. She should be back soon. In the meantime why don't I put them in water? They look like they're starting to wilt."

"It's hot as blazes out."

"I know. It was pretty warm and sticky when we took our walk this morning. Do you have a vase?"

He shrugged. "I recall Ms. Densmore setting out fresh flowers, but if there is a vase I have no idea where it would be."

He followed her to the kitchen, where she began to search for something to put the flowers in.

"Whatever you're making, it smells delicious."

"It's some sort of Mexican casserole, but I can't take credit. Joy said she was tired of carryout. But I'll warn you that it's vegetarian."

He didn't care, as long as it tasted good.

Because frankly, he was tired of carryout, too. He'd been spoiled by Ms. Densmore's home-cooked meals and the five-star dinning that he'd grown used to.

He opened the fridge and grabbed a beer, noticing that someone had even cleaned out the food that had begun to spoil. "The apartment looks great, by the way."

"Also thanks to Joy," she said, rising up on her toes to peer in the cabinet above the refrigerator. "She went through here like a maniac this morning."

He twisted the cap off his beer and took a long pull. "She doesn't strike me as the type who would like to clean."

"You wouldn't think it to look at her, but Joy is far more domestically gifted than I am," she said, going through another cupboard with no luck. "She says it relieves stress. And she was pretty stressed out today."

"Is she nervous about the film role?"

"No, apparently the much older guy that she was living with decided to move his wife back in, so she's got nowhere to live and no job when she goes back to L.A."

"What is she going to do?"

Sierra shrugged. "Joy is twenty-two. It's time she started taking responsibility for herself. She can't be the reckless kid any longer."

Joy may have been a bit irresponsible, but she was still family. He knew from personal experience that pursuing dreams took sacrifice, and it sounded as if this film role was the break she had been working toward. He knew Sierra wasn't in a position to help her out, and though he knew she would never ask him to help Joy, he could. In fact, he had a pretty good idea how he could do it, without actually appearing to do it.

Sierra finally found the vases in the very back of one of the lower cabinets and pulled out two. "These should work."

She set them on the countertop, then turned to him. "I almost forgot, how did your meeting go?"

"The deal fell through."

"What! What happened?"

He told her how Norris had raised his price and that he had turned him down. "Ben seems to think that he'll come around, but I'm not holding my breath."

"I'm so sorry, Coop. I know how much you wanted this."

"I'm more concerned about the guys on the team. Since Norris took over he's been running the team into the ground. They were counting on me to turn things around."

"They're your friends. They respect you. I'm sure they'll understand."

"I hope so."

As she was filling the vases with water the front door opened and Joy stepped inside, weighed down with more plastic grocery bags than one person should carry. Coop set his beer down and rushed over to help her. "I hope Sierra gave you money out of the house account for all this," he said, carrying several bags to the kitchen.

"Since I'm broke and my shoplifting days are over—" she set her bags down on the granite with a thunk "—she had no choice."

"Look what Coop got you," Sierra said, dropping Joy's bouquet into a vase.

"Well, damn, wasn't that sweet of you." Joy leaned close and inhaled the scent of the blooms. "They're lovely. Thanks."

"Originally I bought them to say congratulations, but I think they work better as a thank-you for cleaning the apartment and cooking dinner."

"It's the least I can do. Besides," she added, shooting Sierra a wry smile, "you've probably noticed my sister isn't much of a housekeeper. Or a cook."

Sierra gave her a playful jab in the arm. "And let's see you balance a checkbook or pay your rent on time."

"Gotta find a place to live before I can pay rent, don't I?"

She had just given him the perfect segue. "Sierra mentioned that your living arrangements have changed, and I wondered if that meant you might not be going back to L.A."

She collapsed on one of the stools, looking thoroughly frustrated. "Honestly, I'm not sure what I'm going to do. I want to go back to L.A., but I might have a better chance finding a job here."

"Can I offer a third option?"

She shrugged. "I'm open to pretty much anything at this point."

"Then how do you feel about Mexico?"

"You think you're pretty sneaky, don't you?" Sierra called to Coop from bed later that night when they were in their room with the door closed. It was still a little strange to think of it as *their* room, but she was feeling more comfortable there. It was decorated in warmer colors than the spare room, with traditionally styled cherrywood furniture, including a king-size bed so huge she could get lost in it. Though there wasn't much chance of that happening, considering that Coop was a cuddler. She was used to sleeping alone, so sharing a bed would take a bit of getting used to, but she couldn't deny the pleasures of waking spooned with a warm, naked and aroused man.

Coop stuck his head out of the bathroom, a

toothbrush wedged in his mouth. "If brushing one's teeth can be considered sneaky," he said around a mouthful of toothpaste.

She shot him a look. "Two weeks in Mexico?"

He grinned. "Oh, *that*."

He was gone again, and she heard the water running, then he walked out of the bathroom.

"You knew Joy didn't have anywhere to go," she said. "And rather than making her figure this out on her own—"

"In my defense, I had already planned to take the trip, and I would have invited her to come with us even if she did have a place in L.A. to go back to." He sat on the edge of the mattress to untie his shoes. "But yes, I'm trying to help her. Is there something wrong with that?"

"I just worry that she's never going to learn to be responsible, to take care of herself."

"She seems to have done okay until now. And following your dream takes sacrifice. That I know from personal experience."

Maybe he had a point. Besides, this way she would get to spend a little more time with Joy because who knew when she would talk to her again?

He kicked his shoes off, peeled off his socks, then stood and pulled his shirt over his head. His jeans went next, then his boxers.

Nice.

He looked so good naked, it was a shame he couldn't walk around like that all the time.

He gathered his clothes and dropped them in the hamper, then he pulled the covers back and slipped into bed beside her. But instead of pulling her into his arms and kissing her, like he normally would, he rolled onto his side facing her, wearing a troubled expression. He'd been unusually quiet all night, and she had a pretty good idea what was on his mind. He'd mentioned the accident report being released and what his lawyer's source had said it contained. And though he had clearly been disturbed, he'd seemed hesitant to discuss it. Maybe because Joy had been there, or maybe he just hadn't been ready to deal with it. But maybe now he was.

She rolled onto her side facing him and asked, "Are you thinking about Ash and Susan?"

He drew in a deep breath and blew it out. "I just keep thinking, there has to be some sort of mistake."

She hated to believe that the people she had entrusted her children to could be so irresponsible, but facts were facts. If the report said there were drugs in their systems, then there probably were.

"I *know* Ash," Coop said. "He just wouldn't do something like that."

And she knew for a fact that he didn't know everything about Ash. Everyone had secrets and did things that they weren't proud of. Everyone made mistakes.

"If it had been faulty equipment or turbulent weather..." He shook his head. "But pilot error? It just seems so senseless. How could he do that to Susan and the girls?"

"And you?"

"*Yes,* and me. After all we went through losing our parents, why would he put me through that again? I'm just so damned...*angry.*"

"I felt the same way about my mom."

"But she got sick. She couldn't help that."

"Actually, she could have. Joy doesn't know this, and I don't ever want her to know, but I overheard my dad talking to his sister a few months after the funeral. My mom had a cyst in her breast a couple of years earlier but it turned out to be benign. So when she found another lump, she assumed it was a cyst again."

"But it wasn't."

She shook her head. "By the time she went to the doctor, it had already metastasized. It was in her lungs and her bones. There really wasn't much they could do."

"And if she had gone in as soon as she found the lump?"

"Statistically, there's a seventy-three-percent chance she would be alive today. I was *so* angry at her, but being mad wouldn't bring her back. It just made me really miserable." She reached over and touched Coop's arm. "I'm sure your brother didn't get into that plane thinking that something like this would happen. People make mistakes."

"Come here," he said. She scooted closer and he wrapped his arms around her, pulling her against him chest to chest, bare skin against bare skin. Nice.

She closed her eyes and laid her head in the crook of his neck.

"I just want this to be over, so I can get on with my life," he said.

"It doesn't always work that way."

"I miss him."

"I know."

He buried his face against her hair, holding on so tight it was hard to breathe. "He was all I had left."

"You have the twins. They need you."

"And I need them. I never realized how much having a child could change a man. I'm a better person because of them."

She pulled back so she could see his face. "You said before that you were worried you would let Susan and Ash down, but you've done such an awesome job with the twins. They would be so proud of you." She couldn't imagine being separated from the girls, but if that ever happened, she felt confident that they would be well taken care of. Coop would be a good dad. All the more reason for him not to know the truth. She didn't want to risk changing the way he felt about the girls. And yes, her, too.

"This is probably a really weird time to ask this," he said. "But what are your feelings on prenuptial agreements?"

The timing was a little weird. And it was the second time that week that he'd brought up the subject of marriage. "I haven't really given it much thought," she said. "I've never come close to getting married, and even if I had, the men I date aren't exactly rolling in money."

"But if someone asked you to sign one?"

He looked conflicted, as if he didn't really want to be talking about this. He had seen his attorney that morning, so she could only assume the subject had come up. Which meant he was discussing marrying her with other people now. That had to be a good sign, right?

She hadn't wanted to let herself believe it could really happen. She didn't want to get her hopes up only to have them crushed. But it was looking as though he was seriously planning to marry her. Why discuss a prenup with his attorney if he wasn't?

"I guess it would depend on who was asking," she said.

"What if *I* was asking?"

She shrugged. "I would say sure."

"You wouldn't be upset or hurt?"

"Considering what you're worth, I would think you were a moron if you didn't ask for one. I know you would be fair. And maybe you haven't noticed, but I'm not interested in your money."

A slow smile crept across his face. "Have I ever mentioned what an amazing woman you are?"

If he knew the truth, he may not think she was all that amazing. Learning that his brother may have been under the influence of drugs while flying would be nothing compared to the bombshell she could drop on him. And in this case, what he didn't know really couldn't hurt him. So what was the harm in keeping a secret that he had no chance in ever learning? Why, when things were so good, would she risk rocking the boat?

And if she was so sure it was okay, why did she feel so guilty? Would she ever be able to completely relax with Coop, or would she always feel the nagging feeling of something unsettled between them?

But then Coop pulled her closer, trailed kisses from her lips to her throat and down to her breasts, awakening a passion that she'd felt with no one before him. Like he said before, nothing that felt this good could be wrong. And some things were better left unsaid.

The last month had been the most blissful, most relaxing of Sierra's life. Coop's beachfront condo in Cabo San Lucas was like an oasis. And being out of the States and away from the media seemed to soften the blow of the NTSB report, which was just as bad as Ben's source had predicted.

She and Coop spent their days walking along the beach or lounging by the pool, and the twins were like little mermaids in their matching swimsuits and floating rings. They *loved* the water, howling pitifully whenever she and Coop took them out. But with all the sun and activity, they were so exhausted by evening, they began to sleep peacefully through the night, leaving the adults plenty of alone time.

They spent their evenings out on the patio sipping wine and snacking on the local fare, and after dark they built bonfires. A few days after they arrived they met a young couple from Amsterdam, Joe and Trina, who were renting a neighboring condo and had a son close to the twins' age. For the next week both the kids and the parents became inseparable. Coop and Joe went golfing together while Sierra and Trina played with the kids by the pool or took them into the village to shop. The week flew by, and everyone was disappointed when Joe and Trina had to leave.

Sierra had hoped that the trip would mean spending some quality time with her sister, but Joy being Joy, she met a man and spent a considerable part of her time with him at his condo about a quarter of a mile down the shore.

When their two weeks were drawing to an end, no one felt ready to leave, and because Coop had no pressing business back in New York, he suggested they stay a third week. Then three weeks became four, and by the time they flew home—with Joy remaining in Mexico until she had to leave for Vancouver—July was practically over.

Everyone missed the sun and the beach and especially the pool. The twins were so despondent at first that Coop suggested they consider looking for a home upstate. Maybe something on a lake with a huge yard for the girls to play in and of course a pool. Sierra hadn't been sure if he was completely serious, but then he disappeared into his office and came out an hour later with a stack of real estate listings that he had printed out.

Life with Coop was more perfect than she could have imagined, and she was happier and more content than she'd ever been. But as close as she and Coop had become, she knew that deep inside she was holding something back. She loved Coop, but she still hadn't said the words. Of course, he hadn't said them, either, or brought up the subject of marriage again, but he'd shown his affection for her in a million other ways. She couldn't expect a man like Coop, who had never even had a steady relationship, to go all gooey and lovesick in his first few months out of the gate. These things took time. Maybe she was holding back because she didn't want to rush him, didn't want to make him feel as though he had to commit to feelings he wasn't quite ready to express. Or maybe she was holding back because of the secrets she couldn't bring herself to tell him.

"What do you think of this one?" Coop asked the week after they returned from their trip. The twins were down for their nap and Coop had called her into his office. He pulled her down into his lap so she could see the listing on his ginormous computer monitor.

"It just went on the market yesterday, and the Realtor thinks it's a great price for the area and probably won't be available for long."

The house itself was gorgeous. Big and beautiful and modern, with all the amenities they were looking for, and when she saw the listing price she practically swallowed her own tongue. "It's so expensive."

He shrugged. "It's half of what this place cost me. And after we settle into the house I'll put this place on the market. So technically I'll actually make money. The Realtor can take us through this afternoon. Maybe Lita can watch the kids for a couple of hours and we can go just the two of us.

Lita was the housekeeper Coop had hired right before they left for Cabo. She had taken care of the apartment while they were gone, and since they returned the twins had taken an immediate shine to her. Even better, she absolutely adored them. Her English wasn't the best, but she kept the apartment spotless, she was a decent cook, and most important, she had a very pleasant disposition. And having raised six kids of her own, she was also an experienced babysitter.

"Unless you don't like the house," Coop said, "In which case we'll keep looking."

"It looks really nice, but what I think doesn't really matter. You're buying it, not me."

"No, *we're* buying it. It's going to be your house as much as mine."

She wished that were true, but until they were married, it was his dime. No community property, no alimony if it didn't work out.

Coop shook his head and rubbed a hand across his jaw. "You don't believe me."

"It has nothing to do with me believing you."

"Then you don't trust me."

"It's not about that, either. We're living together, but technically we're still just dating. If you buy a house, it's going to be *your* house."

"Because we're not married."

She nodded.

"Well, maybe we should get married."

It took a second to process the meaning of his words. Had he really just asked her to marry him? She opened her mouth to reply, but no sound came out. She didn't know what to say.

Was he seriously asking, or just throwing out suggestions?

"Is that a no?"

Oh, my God, he was asking, and he expected an answer. "Of course it isn't, I just—"

"Look," he said, turning her in his lap so he could look into her eyes, taking her hands in his and holding them gently. "I know this is hard for you. I know you have trust issues, and I've been trying really hard to give you space, to not overwhelm you, but I'm getting tired of holding back. I love you, Sierra. I know it's only been two months, but it's been the happiest two months of my life. I want to marry you and spend the rest of my life with you. I want us to adopt the girls together and be a real family. If it happens next week, or next year, I don't care. I just need to know that we're on the same page, that you want that, too."

More than he could imagine. "I do want that, and I had no idea you felt that way. I fell in love with you the first time you kissed me. I just didn't say anything because I didn't want to overwhelm *you.* I might have trust issues but not with you."

He grinned, sliding his arms around her. "Sounds like we had a slight breakdown of communication."

She looped her arms around his neck. "I guess we did."

"Let's promise that from now on, we tell each other exactly what we're feeling, that we don't hold anything back."

"I think that's a good idea."

He gave her a soft, sweet kiss. "So, if your answer isn't no…"

"Yes, I'll marry you."

He pulled her close and held her tight.

She loved Coop, and she wanted this, more than anything in her life. She thought about what Joy said, that they couldn't base this relationship on lies. But the truth could tear them apart forever.

Fourteen

Things were moving fast, but Coop liked it that way.

He rolled over in bed and reached for Sierra, but her side of the bed was cold. He squinted at the clock and was surprised to see that it was almost nine, which meant Sierra and the twins were probably taking their morning walk. And he needed to get his butt out of bed. They had a long, busy day ahead of them. After a week of negotiating, they would find out this morning if the sellers of the house they wanted had come back with a reasonable offer. After lunch they had a meeting planned with a wedding coordinator—one who came highly recommended from several of the players' wives—and after that Coop and Sierra were going ring shopping. They had been scouring the Internet for a week, trying to find the perfect one with no luck. She decided that if she was actually seeing them in person, putting them on her finger, something might click. They had a list of a dozen or so places in the city to look, including Cartier, Verdura and of course Tiffany's.

Coop pushed himself out of bed, showered and dressed, then wandered out to the kitchen, surprised to find Lita sitting on the living room floor playing with the twins.

"Good morning, Lita. Where is Miss Evans?"

"Morning, Mr. Landon. She have appointment. She say she leave note for you, on your desk."

"Thanks."

He gave the twins each a kiss on the tops of their heads, then poured himself a cup of coffee and carried it to his office.

He found Sierra's note on his desk by the phone. It said that Ben had called and needed him to call back ASAP. He had been drafting a prenup, even though Coop was still opposed to the idea, but Sierra had insisted.

He sat at his desk and dialed Ben's number.

"Are you sitting down?" Ben asked.

"Actually, yeah, why?"

"I got a call from Mike Norris's lawyer this morning. He wants to talk deal."

Coop's heart stalled in his chest. "You told him I won't budge on price?"

"He knows. Apparently Mike just wants to sell. It would seem that the players have been giving him a bit of a hard time lately."

Coop smiled. He had been worried that they would be angry, but instead they had rallied around him. They knew exactly what Norris was doing and they were pissed.

"When do they want to meet?" Coop asked.

"Tomorrow at three."

"Make it eleven—that way, when the deal is locked in, you and I can go out for lunch to celebrate."

"I'll let him know. Maybe you can come a little early and look over the final draft of the prenup. We made all the changes you asked for, although I still think you're being a little too generous."

"I know what I'm doing."

"I hope so."

He hung up wearing a grin. He had a hunch that Norris would come around, but until just now he hadn't let himself get his hopes up. He still didn't want to count his chickens, but it did sound as if Norris was ready to accept his offer. Everything was falling into place. Personally and professionally. It was almost too good to be true.

He glanced over at the boxes lining one wall of his office. Susan's mother had sent them over after she packed up Ash and Susan's belongings. Things she thought Coop would want. He hadn't been ready to deal with what he would find inside them, especially after reading the NTSB report. But Sierra had been right—being angry at Ash was irrational and counterproductive.

He walked over, grabbed one of the boxes and carried it to his desk. He took a slow, deep breath, telling himself it's like a Band-Aid. You just have to rip it off.

He grabbed the edge of the packing tape and ripped. He opened the flaps, and inside he found a stack of wrapped photo frames. One by one he pulled them from the box and extracted them from the packing. He found photos of Ash and Susan and the girls together. Photos of Ash and Coop with their parents from holidays and vacations, and a 5x7 of Ash and Coop at Coop's high school graduation—Coop in his cap and gown and Ash standing beside him, beaming like a proud parent.

Swallowing back an acute sting of sorrow, he set the photo aside to hang on his office wall.

At the very bottom of the box he found the twins' baby book. Smiling, he lifted it out and flipped through the pages. At the front there were pages and pages of prebirth information, filled in, he was assuming, by the birth mother. Then there was a section recording the events of the girls' first few months, and that was in Susan's handwriting. It contained their growth charts, their sleep and eating schedules, the date of their first smile and the first time eating cereal. A couple of months ago he would have seen keeping such details as a silly waste of time, but now he found himself engrossed.

He sat at his desk sipping his coffee and reading the pages Susan had filled in, which ended abruptly after the girls turned five months. He was assaulted by guilt for not continuing on the tradition, realizing that some day the twins would probably want to look back at it, maybe even show it to their children.

He vowed that, starting today, he would go back and fill in as much information as possible from those missed months, then keep the book up to date from now on. He was sure Sierra would help him. She would remember the finer details he'd forgotten or overlooked.

Curious about the woman who gave birth to the girls, he flipped back to the beginning. He couldn't find her name, which was no surprise, and though there were a few photos of her pregnant belly, they were all from the chest down. Yet as he thumbed through the pages, reading the pregnancy milestones, he was overwhelmed with an eerie sense of déjà vu. He was sure he'd read this before. It just looked so…familiar. He racked his memory, wondering if maybe he'd seen the baby book at Ash and Susan's place. But he was sure he hadn't. Even if it had been sitting right in front of him he wouldn't have thought to pick it up. So why did it look so familiar?

Realization hit him like a stick check to the gut, knocking the air from his lungs. No way. It wasn't possible.

He snatched the note Sierra had left him from the trash beside his desk and compared it to the writing in the baby book, and the coffee he'd just swallowed threatened to rise back up his throat. It was identical. Completely and totally identical.

Sierra, the woman he loved and planned to marry, was the girls' birth mother.

Sierra opened the apartment door, her hair clinging to her damp forehead. It was a hot, sticky morning headed toward a blistering hot afternoon. She went right to the kitchen, poured herself a glass of cold water from the fridge and guzzled it down. Then she went down the hall in search of Lita and the girls. She found them in the nursery in the middle of a diaper change.

"I'm back, Lita. Is Mr. Landon still here?"

"He in his office," she said, concern furrowing her brow. "I go to talk to him, but he look angry."

Which probably meant that their offer on the house had been turned down. Well, shoot. They had seen a dozen different places in the past week, but that was by far their favorite. Coop was going to be so disappointed.

The past week, since she said she would marry him, had been a bit of a whirlwind. He seemed determined to get them married and settled into a house as fast as humanly possible. As if he were trying to make it official before she had a chance to get away. He had even mentioned that if they were going to have more children, he wanted to do it soon, so they would be close in age. She already had her hands pretty full with the twins, but he seemed to want it so badly she didn't have the heart to say she wanted to wait a while.

She felt a little like she was on a speeding train, and even if she wanted off, it was moving too fast to jump.

Sierra walked to Coop's office. The door was closed so she rapped lightly.

"Come in."

She opened the door and stepped inside. Coop was standing by the window, looking out, hands wedged in the pockets of his jeans.

"Hey, is everything okay? Lita said you looked angry."

"Close the door," he said, not looking at her.

Something definitely was wrong. She snapped the door shut and asked, "Coop, what's the matter? Did the Realtor call? Did they turn down our offer?"

"They didn't call yet. I finally started going through one of the boxes of Ash's things."

No wonder he was upset. "Oh, Coop. That must have been really hard."

"I found a whole bunch of photos, and the twins' baby book. It's on my desk."

She walked over to his desk. A stack of framed photographs sat on one corner, and next to it, the baby book she hadn't seen in almost seven months.

"I bookmarked my favorite page. Have a look."

She picked it up and thumbed through it until she found the page, marked with the note she'd written him this morning. She saw the writing on the note and the writing on the page, and her stomach bottomed out. Side by side they were clearly identical. Her knees went so limp she had to sink down into the chair.

She looked up to see that Coop had turned and was glaring down at her, his eyes so cold she nearly shivered.

"That's your handwriting. You're the twins' birth mother."

She closed her eyes and drew in a shaky breath. Joy was right. She should have told him.

"Nothing to say?" he asked, and the anger simmering just below the surface made her heart skip.

"I can explain."

"Don't bother. Here's what I think happened. You wanted them back, but I refused to give them up and you knew you didn't have a shot in hell in court. So instead you decided to infiltrate my home, to prove me unfit."

"No, Coop——"

"But then you looked around and realized what a sweet life you could have as my wife, so you seduced me instead."

"It wasn't like that at all. I just needed to know that they were okay. Your reputation... I didn't know what kind of parent you would be. I was scared. I thought they needed me. I swear, I never intended to act as anything but their nanny. And I never wanted anything from you. You know that."

"Did you ever plan to tell me the truth?"

She could tell him she did, that she was waiting for the right time, but that would be a lie. "I was afraid to."

"Because you thought I would be angry? And feel betrayed? Well, you were right."

"It wasn't that. At least, not entirely. I was afraid it would change the way you felt about the twins. You're so good with them, and you love them so much. I thought it might change your feelings toward them. And yes, toward me."

"So you just planned to lie to me, what, for the rest of our lives?"

"You'll never know how hard it's been keeping the truth from you. And if I thought for a second that you would understand, I would have told you that very first day. But look at it from my point of view. I didn't know you. All I knew is what I read in the papers and heard on the news. I didn't even know that you had any interest in taking care of twins who you believed you weren't technically related to."

His eyes narrowed. "What do you mean, who I *believed* I wasn't related to?"

Damn it. Had she really just said that?

"Sierra?"

Damn, damn, *damn.*

It was one thing not to tell him and another to lie about it. Besides, he was bound to ask about the birth father some day, and not telling him would be another lie. "Coop, you're the girls' uncle."

"I know that."

"No, I mean that you are the girls' *biological* uncle. Ash wasn't just Fern and Ivy's adoptive dad. He was their birth dad."

The room seemed to tilt on its axis and Coop clutched the edge of the desk for support. "You *slept* with my brother."

"Yes, but it's not what you're thinking."

"You have *no idea* what I'm thinking."

"Please," she said, looking desperate, "give me a chance to explain."

Nothing she could say could take away the sick feeling in his stomach, in his soul. Ash had cheated on Susan. On top of being responsible for killing himself and his wife, Ash, who Coop had considered beyond reproach, had committed adultery. It was as if everything he knew about his brother was a lie.

"I met Ash in a bar."

"Ash didn't hang out in bars."

"And neither did I, but I had just put my father in a nursing home and I felt horrible, and I didn't feel like sitting home alone, so I stopped in for a drink. I just happened to sit beside him at the bar, and we were both drinking vodka tonics, and we got to talking. He said he was there because he and his wife were separating. He told me that they had been having fertility issues for years and after another failed IVF attempt, it was just too much."

Coop knew they had been trying to get pregnant for a while, but Ash never said anything about any negative effects on his marriage. If he and Susan had been separating, he would have said something to Coop. "I don't believe you."

"It's the truth."

"So why didn't he tell me?"

She shrugged. "I don't know. Maybe he was embarrassed? Maybe it was easier to talk to a stranger. All I know is that he had come from his lawyer's office, and they were going to sign papers the next morning. If you don't believe me, I'm sure his lawyer could confirm it. I'm sure with them gone he would waive privilege."

He would be sure to check that. "So you met in a bar..."

"We talked for a long time and had a few drinks too many, and we ended up back at my place. It was a mistake. We both knew it right afterward. He called me the next day to apologize and to tell me that what happened between us had knocked some sense into him. He and Susan had talked and were going to try to work things out. He begged me not to say anything to her, and of course I wouldn't. He was a great guy, and I was really happy for him. But a couple of weeks later I found out I was pregnant. I called him, and of course he was stunned and heartbroken. He wanted a child so badly, but to be in the baby's life he would have to admit to Susan what he'd done, and that would ruin his marriage."

"He would never do that. He would never refuse to take responsibility for his own child."

"He wanted to, but how would he explain the missing money? He said that Susan handled all of their finances. Things were already really tight. The fertility treatments were drain-ing them financially."

If things were that bad, why hadn't he asked Coop for help? Coop *owed* him. He could have been the one to pay the support. Ash had made a mistake, and he should have owned up to it.

"It was a really terrible time for me to be having a baby. I was barely scraping by as it was, and I would have had to put the baby in day care while I worked seventy hours a week. I started to think about adoption, and when I found out I was having twins, I knew I couldn't keep them. I couldn't give them the sort of life they deserved. But I knew who could. I figured if the twins couldn't be with their mother, they could at least be with their dad."

"So why did Ash have to adopt his own kids?"

"He came up with the adoption idea so Susan wouldn't know about the affair. He was so afraid of losing her."

"And you just went along with this. You just gave up your babies to save a virtual stranger's marriage."

"I didn't have a choice. It was an impossible situation. Without his help, I couldn't keep them, and he couldn't give me any financial help without ruining his marriage. Giving them up was the hardest thing I ever had to do, but I did it because it was best for them."

"You must have been pretty happy when you heard about the crash, knowing you would get the chance to be with them again."

Tears welled in her eyes. "That's a terrible thing to say. And it's not true. If I didn't think they would have a good life with Ash and Susan, I never would have suggested the adoption. I would have given them to some other family who was desperate for children."

"You know what I find ironic? All this time I knew something wasn't right. I chocked it up to you having trust issues, when all along you were the one lying, the one who couldn't be trusted."

"I know it was wrong to lie to you, but I didn't have a choice. I didn't expect to fall in love with you. It's not something I planned, and I fought it. You know I did."

"Or that's what you wanted me to believe."

"It's the truth."

"What difference does it make now? It's over. I won't ever be able to trust you again."

She lowered her eyes, wringing her hands in her lap. "I know. And I'm sorry."

"And to think I was willing to marry you without a prenup. That's the last time I question my lawyer's advice." And he didn't doubt for a second that her insistence in signing one was all a part of her scheme. And what if he had married her? What if they'd had a child? The thought made his stomach ache.

"You didn't deserve this," she said. "And I know you won't believe this, but I do love you."

"You're right. I don't believe you."

She rose to her feet, her face pale, looking like she might either be sick or lose consciousness. "I'll go pack."

He laughed. "You don't seriously think I'm going to let you off that easy, let you leave your daughters?"

She blinked, confusion in her eyes. "But...I thought..."

"I may think that you're a miserable human being, but they need you. Do you really think I would rip them away from the only mother they have? But don't think for a second that you are anything but an employee."

"You want me to stay? *Here?*"

"Obviously you're moving back into your bedroom. And I'm going to treat you like the servant that you are. And you're going to take a substantial pay cut."

"You don't think it will be awkward, me staying here?"

"Oh, I'm counting on it. It's going to be that nightmare scenario you mentioned when you were telling me all the supposed reasons why you didn't want to get involved. You are going to live here, day in, day out, watching me get on with my life. Watching me exercise that revolving bedroom door."

"And if I say no? If I quit?"

"You never see the twins again. And you have to live with knowing you abandoned them twice."

She swallowed, tears welling in her eyes

again, but he couldn't feel sorry for her. He flat out refused. She'd made him suffer, and now he was going to return the favor.

"Well then," she said, squaring her shoulders, trying to be strong. "I guess I have no choice but to stay."

Fifteen

Coop had given it considerable thought and had come to the conclusion that he was an idiot.

He sat in his office, staring out the window at nothing, without the motivation to do anything but feel sorry for himself. The past two weeks had been the longest and most miserable of his life. If he thought making Sierra suffer would bring him some sort of satisfaction, he'd been dead wrong. He just wanted her to feel as miserable and betrayed and as *hurt* as he was. But knowing that she was unhappy and hurting was only making him feel worse.

He couldn't concentrate, couldn't sleep.

When he was out with friends he wanted to be home, but when he was home he felt as restless as a caged animal. He didn't want to upend the twins' lives, but living in the same house with Sierra, seeing day to day how guilty and unhappy she felt, was killing him.

The worst part was that this was just as much his fault as hers. Probably more.

Deep down he had known there was something wrong, that something was just slightly… off. And instead of bothering to try to identify its real source, he'd passed it off as her shortcoming and left it at that, thinking that as soon as she accepted how wonderful he was she would be the perfect companion. When, in reality, he was the one with the bigger problem. He had lousy vision. He saw only what he wanted to see. He had pursued her with a single-minded determination that was almost manic. She'd resisted, and he'd ignored her. She pushed back, he insisted. He hadn't *let* her tell him no.

Looking back, he couldn't help but wonder what the hell he'd been thinking. Moving her into his bedroom after two weeks and planning a wedding six weeks after that. If she'd been pregnant he maybe could have understood the urgency. And speaking of that, the stretch marks should have tipped him off that there might be something she wasn't telling him. He had just assumed that she had been a little overweight at some point and they were the result. It wasn't the sort of thing a man could ask a woman. Not without getting slugged. Or so he wanted to believe. He never really asked her about her past. The truth was, he didn't want to know. It had been easier just to pretend that she was perfect, that her life didn't really begin until she met him.

What a selfish, arrogant jerk he'd been.

Though it had taken a little time to realize it, it wasn't even Sierra who was making him so angry. How could Ash, who had drilled into Coop the virtues of being a responsible adult and a good man, be so careless and self-centered? He should have supported Sierra, his marriage be damned. He should have owned up to the responsibility, so she could keep the babies, so they could be with their mother, where they belonged. Instead he had ripped them from her arms and taken them for himself. Coop didn't think he would ever understand it or ever be able to forgive him for what he'd done.

Yes, Sierra had lied to him but only because she thought she was doing what was best for her children. They were her number-one priority, as they should be. She was a good mother. She'd made more sacrifices for those girls than most women would ever consider. And he intended to make sure they knew it.

Ironically, now that he knew who Sierra was, warts and all, he loved her more than he had two weeks ago when he had her built up in his mind as the perfect mate. But after the way he'd treated her, why would she ever want him back? He told her that he loved her, that he wanted to spend the rest of his life with her, and at the first sign of trouble, he'd bailed on her. How could she love someone who had failed her so completely? And how could she ever trust that he wouldn't do it again?

He had really hoped by now that she would have come crawling to him on her knees begging for forgiveness, in which case he wouldn't have to admit what an utter jerk he'd been. Clearly that wasn't going to happen. He needed her a whole lot more than she needed him. Or maybe she just believed it was hopeless and didn't want to risk being rejected again.

He heard the doorbell ring and knew that it was Vlad, Niko and a few other guys from the team. Coop had met with Norris, who after some balking had agreed to their original terms. The deal was in place, and in just a few weeks Coop would officially be the new owner, so the guys wanted to celebrate. This deal had been all he could think about for months, yet now that he'd gotten what he wanted, he couldn't work up the will to be excited about it. It was as if losing Sierra had sucked the life right out of him.

Lita poked her head in his office. "Your guests is here, sir."

"Serve them drinks and I'll be right there."

She nodded and backed out.

He had no choice but to go out there and pretend as if everything was fine. But it wasn't, and wouldn't be, until Sierra was his again. And she would be. He would get her back. He just didn't have a clue how to go about it.

Sierra ignored the doorbell and read the girls their bedtime story. She had overheard Coop telling Lita—who seemed hopelessly confused by Sierra's abrupt switch from lady of the house to employee—that he was having a few guys from the team over. Was this him finally getting on with his life? Because she had been waiting, and other than a night out with friends in which he came home alone at an unimpressive nine-thirty and a couple of business meetings, he'd spent most of the past two weeks holed up in his office.

When it came to dishing out revenge, he wasn't very good at it.

That didn't mean she wasn't miserable and unhappy, and she missed him so much every cell in her body ached with it. Yet she couldn't deny the feeling that some enormous, cloying weight had been lifted from her, and for the first time in months she could actually breathe again. She realized now that if she had married Coop with that secret between them, she never would have been able to relax. She would have forever felt as though she didn't deserve him because everything that he knew about her was essentially a lie.

Unfortunately, the one thing that could have saved their relationship, *the truth,* had been the thing that killed it. Just like her pregnancy, it had been a lose-lose situation from the start, and she had been a fool for letting herself believe that it would work. For thinking that he wouldn't eventually learn the truth. And that it would end in anything but total disaster.

If he could ever find a way to forgive her, she would never lie to him again. But it seemed unlikely that would ever happen. He hated her, and that really sucked, but at least he knew the truth.

From the other room she heard men's voices. No doubt they would go up on the roof, drink and talk about what a waste of time she had been and the compromising position he had managed to trap her into.

Because she was in no mood for a confrontation with Coop's pals, she read the twins a second then a third book, realizing halfway through that they were out cold. She laid them in bed, grabbed their empty bottles and walked to the kitchen. Lita had already left for the night, and the dishwasher was running, so she dropped the bottles in the sink and washed them by hand.

She was setting them on a towel to dry when she heard the sound of footsteps behind her, but the cloying scent of aftershave tipped her off to the source. She turned to find Niko standing behind her.

"I need beer," he said, setting an empty beer bottle on the counter.

Was he just stating fact, or was he expecting her to wait on him? She was the nanny, not Coop's hostess. His friends could serve themselves, which Niko did.

"Coop tell us it's over," he said, walking past her to the fridge and pulling out a beer.

Normally she didn't feel threatened by the younger Russian, but there was something in the way he looked at her tonight. His eyes roamed over her in a way that made her feel dirty.

"That's right," she said.

He stepped closer. "I like sister, maybe I like you, too."

Oh, yuck. "I'm not interested."

She turned to the sink and felt a very large palm settle on her butt. Repulsion roiled her stomach. And she couldn't help wondering if Coop had put him up to this, if that was part of her humiliation. But before she could turn and slap his hand away, it was gone. She spun around to see Coop pulling the Russian away from her, then he drew his arm back and punched him square in the jaw. Actually *punched* him.

Niko's head snapped back and he lost his balance, landing on his ass on the ceramic tile floor.

If he put Niko up to it, then why punch him?

Niko muttered something in Russian that

Sierra was guessing was a curse and rubbed his jaw. He looked more annoyed than angry.

"What the hell is wrong with you?" Coop said.

"You say you and her is finished. So I think, why not?"

Coop glared at the Russian, then looked over at Sierra and said, "Are you okay?"

"Fine." Just mildly disgusted.

Coop turned back to Niko, jaw tight, and said, "I'm only going to say this once, so listen clearly and spread the word. The only man who's going to be touching this woman's ass is *me*."

Niko shrugged and pulled himself to his feet. "Okay, fine, jeez. I look but I don't touch."

"No, you don't get to look, either. Or *think* about looking."

Sierra planted her hands on her hips. "Excuse me, but do I have any say in this, since it is *my* ass we're talking about."

He pointed to Niko. "You, back to the terrace." He turned to Sierra. "You, bedroom, *now*."

What did he think, he could just order her

around? And if he couldn't, why, as he stomped down the hall to his bedroom, was she following him? Maybe because the fact that he would punch someone to defend her honor was just a tiny bit flattering. But what she didn't appreciate was the part about him basically owning her. He'd lost that right when he dumped her.

He opened the bedroom door and gestured her inside, and she dumbly complied, but she wasn't a total pushover.

"Look. I don't know who you think you—"

That was as far as she got before Coop spun her around, slanted his mouth over hers and kissed away whatever she'd been about to say. His arms went around her, pulling her hard against him, and instead of fighting it and asking what the heck he thought he was doing, it felt so amazingly wonderful, and she had missed him *so* much, she couldn't help but kiss him back.

So much for not being a pushover.

He kicked the door closed.

"I have been such a jerk," he said. "A miserable excuse for a man. I am so sorry."

She tucked her face against his chest, breathed in deep the scent of him, knowing that she was home. Any reservations that she had been feeling before their fight were gone. "I deserved it."

"No you didn't. And when I saw him touch you…" He squeezed her so hard it was difficult to breathe. "Tell me you didn't like it."

"God, no! It was revolting."

"I don't want another man to ever touch you again. Only me, for the rest of our lives."

She cupped his face in her hands. "You're the only man I want, Coop. The only man I'll ever want. And I am so sorry for what I did. It was killing me having to lie to you. I should have told you the truth from the beginning."

"Sierra, it's okay."

"It's not. I should have come to your door, told you I was the twins' mother and asked you if I could be a part of their lives."

"You never would have made it to my door. The doorman would have to let you up, and he wouldn't have done that without permission from me, and I wouldn't have let you near the twins."

"So you're saying it was okay to lie to you?"

"Maybe not okay, but necessary. If I were in your position, and I thought the twins were in danger, I would have done anything to keep them safe. And what my brother did to you…" He shook his head, as if it was almost too painful to say. "It was so wrong, Sierra. He never should have taken the twins from you. He should have owned up to his responsibility."

"But his marriage—"

"To hell with his marriage. He made a mistake and he should have been man enough to admit it. I love my brother, and I appreciate all the sacrifices he made for me, but I just can't excuse the things he did. I'll never believe it was okay. And I will always take care of you and the twins, the way that he should have."

Her heart sank. She didn't want him to see her as some debt he had to repay. That just wasn't good enough for her anymore. "Because you feel guilty," she said.

He cradled her face in his hands. "No, because I *love* you. I asked you to marry me, and you put your faith in me and the first time things got a little hard I bailed. But it isn't going to happen again. I'm dedicated to making this work. I don't have a choice. I need you too much, love you too much to let you go."

"I love you, too," she said.

"And just so you know, I'm calling my lawyer first thing tomorrow and telling him to tear up the prenup."

Not this again. "But, Coop—"

"I don't need it. And I'm going to tell him to get the ball rolling on having your rights as the twins' mother fully restored."

She sucked in a soft breath. The most she had hoped for was to someday be their adoptive mother. She never thought that she would ever be recognized as their biological mother. "Are you sure, Coop?"

He touched her cheek. "They're your daughters. Of course I'm sure. Then after we're married, I'll adopt them. They'll belong to both of us."

It sounded almost too good to be true, and

this time she wasn't going to take a second of it for granted. "I'm going to be the perfect wife," she told him. "I'll figure out how to cook a decent meal and learn to clean if that's what it takes."

He shook his head. "Nope."

She blinked. "What do you mean?"

"I don't want the perfect wife."

"You don't?"

He grinned down at her, with that sweet, crooked smile—the one she would get to look at for the rest of her life—and said, "I only want you."